PINOCCHIO

In His Own Words

michael morpurgo

PINOCCHIO

In His Own Words

Illustrated by Emma Chichester Clark

HarperCollins *Children's Books*

First published in hardback in Great Britain byHarperCollins *Children's Books* in 2013
Published in this edition 2018
HarperCollins *Children's Books* is a division of HarperCollins*Publishers* Ltd,
77-85 Fulham Palace Road, Hammersmith, London, W6 8JB.

The HarperCollins website address is: www.harpercollins.co.uk

1

Text copyright © Michael Morpurgo 2013
Illustrations copyright © Emma Chichester Clark 2013

ISBN 978-0-00-825769-9

Michael Morpurgo and Emma Chichester Clark assert the moral right
to be identified as the author and illustrator of this work.

Printed and bound in China

To Ann-Janine

*From us both
and from Pinocchio
with our love and thanks.*

Contents

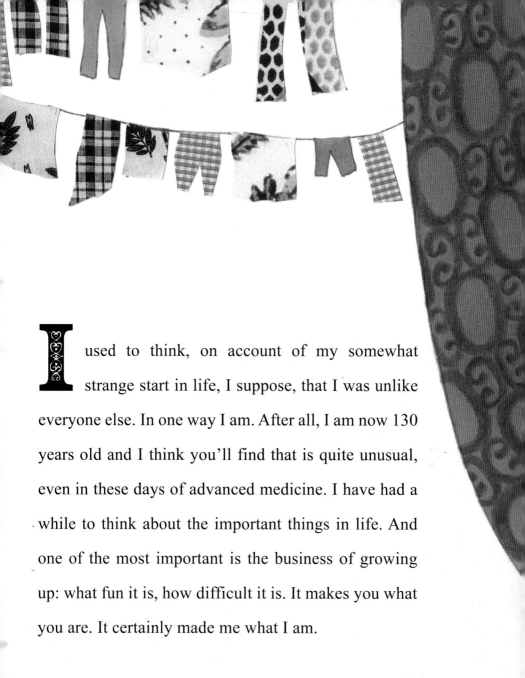

I used to think, on account of my somewhat strange start in life, I suppose, that I was unlike everyone else. In one way I am. After all, I am now 130 years old and I think you'll find that is quite unusual, even in these days of advanced medicine. I have had a while to think about the important things in life. And one of the most important is the business of growing up: what fun it is, how difficult it is. It makes you what you are. It certainly made me what I am.

Now—there's no point in pretending here—I was, and still am deep down, a puppet. Everyone knows Pinocchio is a puppet—Signor Carlo Collodi first told my story, which made me instantly recognizable, and then Mr. Walt Disney made a fantastic film about me, with songs, for goodness' sake; so I reckon I must be just about the most famous puppet the world has ever known.

But the truth is I'm not just a puppet, I'm more than just bits of wood and string. I'm me. So actually I'm quite like you. I mean you're not just skin and hair and flesh and bones, are you? You're you. So, in that sense, if you think about it, we're pretty much the same, aren't we? And we're the same for another reason too. To begin with I may have been just a block of wood about to become a puppet, but you were not much better; just a little wiggly thing, about to become a person. Then we get born, one way or another. It wasn't just the block of wood or the wiggly thing that made us what we are—for better or for worse—it's what we then made of our lives, what happened to us afterwards. So I thought it was about time that I, Pinocchio, told you my story in my own words, not so you can learn from it so much, but so you can see that, no matter what we are made of, we all have an exciting and difficult time growing up.

Anyway, that's the boring part over with. The rest is not at all boring, I can assure you. It will be a roller coaster of danger and disaster, mistakes and misery, hope and happiness. So here it is, the true story, the whole story with nothing left out, of all the pickles I got myself into and out of. You won't know it yet, but when you get older, your childhood will seem like a long dream; sometimes a happy dream, sometimes a bit of a nightmare, sometimes so unlikely you can hardly believe it happened. But it did. You were there, you know. My dream of childhood was just like that. But I know it happened. I was there.

CHAPTER ONE

I get born

So here's how I began. I was a tiny cherry-pip in a blackbird's beak. The blackbird dropped me in an orchard below a town called Naples, and I fell to earth.

After a while, I grew into a fine cherry tree, blossoming wonderfully every year, until one winter's day a raging storm blew me over, and the next thing I know, I am nothing but a piece of wood, a branch in a pile of other branches, waiting to be burnt. And that would have been that. There would have been no Pinocchio.

But…as luck would have it, along came an old woodcarver. He was whistling away as he searched through the pile, and talking to himself. He picked me up, turned me this way and that, peered at me, smelled me even.

"This will do very well," he said. "Cherry-wood, the best for carving. Just what I've been looking for."

He looked about him nervously. "No one's here. No one will notice, will they?" He tapped me with his knuckle, knocked me against a tree. "Yes, you'll carve perfectly."

That was when I spoke my first words—I'd heard a lot of speaking in my life, so words came easily. I'd just never needed them before.

"Excuse me," I said, "but I do wish you wouldn't keep knocking me around like that. It hurts. And carving me up, I'm sure, will hurt a great deal more—I don't like the sound of that one bit."

He heard me. I know that because in his surprise he dropped me on his foot. When he'd stopped hopping about, he began to search, wondering where on earth the voice had come from.

"Anyway, you can't just steal me," I went on.

"All right, all right," he said, clapping his hands to his ears. "I will pay. Here, look. I'm leaving a coin for you on the woodpile."

And with that he tucked me under his arm and legged it. All the way I kept shouting and shouting, begging him to take me back. By the time we reached his house I'd been shouting so loud and for so long that

I'd lost my voice completely.

All around the walls of his house hung the tools of his trade: chisels, planes, hammers, drills. I was terrified. To me they were nothing but instruments of torture. But when I tried protest, nothing would come out, not a squeak, not a whisper. Then I saw the lady sitting by the fire, staring sadly into the flames.

"*Carissima mia*," said the woodcarver. "See what I have for you, my darling."

She turned and looked.

"Not another log," she sighed. "How many times have you tried before? I want a real boy for a son, not a puppet."

"But this is the finest

cherry-wood, *carissima mia*. And when I touch it, it has life. I feel it. I smell it. I can almost hear it. You'll see, my darling. With this piece of wood, I will make you at last the son you have always longed for."

Gepetto's wife shook her head, and I could see there were tears in her eyes. "You are the kindest of men, Gepetto. And I love you because you never stop trying, you never stop hoping. But it is hopeless, I tell you, hopeless. We'll never have a son of our own." And again she turned her face to the fire and wept.

Gepetto the woodcarver took down his tools from the wall, rolled up his sleeves, and wiped his nose with the back of his hand. Then, looking down on me, he said, "I will make a boy of you, block of wood. I will make a son for my darling wife and me. So lie still and be good. It won't hurt."

I was terrified. I tried to yell, I tried to screech, but no sound came out, so of course he heard nothing. But I need not have worried. Gepetto was right. It didn't hurt at all. It felt as if he was tickling me!

My hair, my ears, my forehead—as he worked on them, chiseling them into shape, they simply tickled. I wanted to giggle, to laugh out loud, but I couldn't. And when he made my eyes, I couldn't move them either, not at first. All I could do was stare at him.

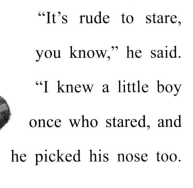

"It's rude to stare, you know," he said. "I knew a little boy once who stared, and he picked his nose too.

He was called Pinocchio. There we are! That shall be your name: Pinocchio! Now for your nose, which you should never pick—because that is ruder even than staring, and *carissima mia* would not like it."

Gepetto had trouble with my nose—it seemed to be too long for my face. But he didn't want to risk cutting it off altogether, so, in the end, he left it too long— something I often blamed him for later on. Children often blame their fathers and mothers later on, it's quite natural.

The real trouble came when he made my mouth. Now I could giggle and laugh, but not out loud yet— because I still had no voice, you remember—but *inside*, and I was killing myself laughing, if you know what I mean. It tickled *so* much. The face was the most complicated part. That's what took the time. After that the neck, the shoulders, the stomach, the legs, the arms, the hands, all came fairly easily.

I could see how excited Gepetto was, how delighted he was with his handiwork. At last, as I lay there on the table, arms and legs outstretched, staring up at him, he stood back, hands on hips, smiling down at me.

"You'll do, Pinocchio," he whispered. "You'll do." Then he picked me up gently in his arms and carried me over to where his wife still sat gazing into the fire, brushing her tears away. He set me on her knee, took her arms and put them around me so that I was cradled in her lap. One large tear fell on my cheek and suddenly I could move, suddenly my voice came back to me too.

"Mama," I cried. "Papa!"

"Pinocchio!" They were both so happy.

Mama held me up higher and then hugged me to

her. They took a hand each to help me walk. But after
going once or twice around the room I didn't need
them any more. Within moments I was walking on my
own, a little wobbly maybe, but not falling over, not
once. Then I was running, running all around the room,
skipping with joy, jumping over the stools. I could
do a split; I could do somersaults; I could stand on
my head!

"Our brave little Pinocchio," Gepetto cried, picking me up and setting me on his shoulder. "We have a son at last, a boy of our own." And together my new Mama and Papa took me out into the streets to show me off to the world.

As word spread around the town, everyone in Naples came running to see me.

"He's not a boy," they shouted, pointing at me and mocking me. "He's just a puppet, a puppet without any strings maybe, but a puppet nonetheless. He can't talk," they cried.

"He can," Gepetto told them triumphantly. "Say something to them, Pinocchio."

"Of course I can talk," I said. "I can walk with no one holding me," I said. And I did. "I can dance," I said. And I did—tap-dancing was easy with wooden feet. "I can do somersaults and handstands too."

They were amazed, everyone was, but they didn't stop laughing at me, and, what was worse, they laughed at Mama and Papa too, who I could tell were so proud of me.

"Look how his wooden head wobbles when he walks! He isn't a real boy," they said. "A real boy has a mind of his own, goes on adventures. You can't make a mind out of wood, Signor Gepetto! He's not a real boy at all. Wobble head! Clumpy feet! Big nose!"

That was it. I'd had enough of all their insults. I took off, sprinted away, did a runner. And could I run! In leaps and bounds I ran, *tickety-tackety tickety-tackety* went my wooden feet on the cobbled streets. They tried to catch me, but I dodged and ducked.

"Grab him!" they shouted. "Catch Pinocchio!" The whole town was after me.

I had almost escaped them when, ahead of me, barring my way, there was a huge, burly policeman, a *Carabiniere*, legs apart, arms wide open to catch me.

Go through his legs, I thought. *It's the only way to get past him.* But he grabbed me by my nose. Can you imagine? The indignity of it!

And then he carried me under his arm, back to Papa and Mama, who took me home at once and put me to bed.

"Never run away again, Pinocchio," Mama said, hugging me tight and kissing me. Then she brought me a mug of hot milk.

"You gave us such a fright," Gepetto said. "We thought we'd lost you for good. No matter what anyone says, you are our dear son, our little boy, and this is your home. Tomorrow you will go to school, like all the other boys and girls."

"What happens at school?" I asked them.

"You will read books and learn to spell and to write and to add and subtract. You will learn to have a mind of your own."

"But I have a mind of my own already," I said. "I

don't like this school idea at all."

"You'll love it," they told me. "You'll soon make lots of friends."

But I didn't love it and I didn't make lots of friends—in fact, not one. All the others did was laugh at me and tease me because I was different. And the teachers were just as bad. The moment they found me staring out of the window dreaming, which was often—I wanted to be out there exploring the world, not stuck in a classroom—they'd put me in the corner with a dunce's cap on my head.

I was standing there in the corner one day when I made up my mind. I knew it would upset Mama and Papa, and I felt bad about that because after all they fed me and looked after me and loved me, but I couldn't stand it any longer. I would run away and see the world. I would make my fortune. I'd show the world I wasn't a puppet, that I was a boy with a mind of my own. I'd make Mama and Papa proud of me, but I'd do it my way.

All right, all right, I know now that it was stupid. But don't think too badly of me. I don't think I was that different from most of you who are reading this—except of course I was made of wood. But that wasn't my fault, was it? I was a wooden-head, a puppet with very little sense. I just wanted to have a good time, do my own thing. That's natural, right?

CHAPTER TWO

One talking cricket... and two smoking feet

Running away, I very soon discovered, has its problems. First of all it rained; it rained cats and dogs, poured down. And then I got hungry, tummy-gurgling hungry. On and on I ran through the rain, down country lanes, past cottages, through villages.

Out of every window wafted scents of baking bread or roasting meat. But whenever I stopped to beg for a morsel of food they shouted at me, told me to go away or they'd sic the dog on me. Some old man with his nightcap on leaned out of his window and bellowed out, "Get lost!"

And because I didn't move, he threw a pail of water all over me. And then because I still wouldn't go—he fired his blunderbuss at me. I had to run then, didn't I?

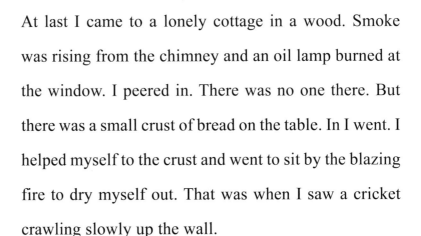

At last I came to a lonely cottage in a wood. Smoke was rising from the chimney and an oil lamp burned at the window. I peered in. There was no one there. But there was a small crust of bread on the table. In I went. I helped myself to the crust and went to sit by the blazing fire to dry myself out. That was when I saw a cricket crawling slowly up the wall.

"*Cri-cri-cri*," he chirruped cheerfully. Then, much to my surprise, he spoke very clearly, very precisely, like my teacher at school. "Running away, little boy, is always a foolish idea. It never makes you happy and it makes your Mama and your Papa very sad."

"What do you know?" I said. "Do you think I want to be like other boys and girls? Do you think I want to learn all that schoolboy stuff? I want to be free, to see the world. I want to run in the woods, chase butterflies, steal birds' eggs. I want to do what I like."

"Go ahead, Pinocchio, and you'll turn into a donkey. Then everyone will laugh at you even more. You have to make something of yourself, earn an honest living. You can't just wander the world. You'll get yourself into all sorts of trouble. You'll end up in prison if you're not careful."

His lecture went on and on. *Don't do this. Do that, or else.*

I'd had quite enough. "I don't need lessons from a stupid talking cricket. Stop it, stop it right now or you'll be sorry."

But he didn't stop. "Oh, Pinocchio," he sighed, "I am so sorry for you."

"Why?"

"Because you're a puppet, because inside your wooden head you have no sense at all. I fear you are going to have to learn the hard way."

I knew I shouldn't have done it. In my fury I picked up a log and hurled it at him. I didn't mean to kill him, just to frighten him, to shut him up.

But my aim was too good.

"*Cri-cri-cri*," he cried, and fell down lifeless on the floor.

Murderer! Murderer! cried a little voice in my head. *You are a murderer, Pinocchio.*

I lay down and sobbed, begging forgiveness of the poor cricket. But then I felt hungry again—the bread crust had hardly been enough—and very soon I felt a lot less sorry for the cricket. All I could think about was food. I scoured the cottage, searching high and low for something to eat, anything.

Imagine my joy when I spotted an egg nestling on a bed of straw, a perfect big brown egg. I kissed and fondled it, sang to it. Yes, I sang to an egg—I was that hungry. "Oh, you beautiful thing, you great big beautiful thing!"

I had seen Mama cooking eggs. I knew what to do. I boiled some water on the stove, and set the egg in gently so as not to break it. Four minutes for a nice soft egg. I counted the seconds, longing to taste that scrumptious golden yolk, "forty-eight, forty-nine, fifty!"

On the count of fifty, to my amazement, the egg cracked open and before my eyes out popped a golden chick. She flew up from the saucepan and landed on the table.

"So kind of you to open me up, Signor Pinocchio. I could never have been born without you. Bless your heart, you're a good, kind puppet!" And cheeping happily she ran off out of the door, flapping her little golden wings.

My supper was escaping and there was nothing I could do about it. I sat down in front of the fire feeling very stupid indeed.

"You stupid, stupid wooden-head," I told myself. "You ran away from home where there was always food aplenty, where you had a Mama and a Papa who loved you; you killed a poor cricket who was only telling you the truth and trying to help you. Will you never learn? That poor old cricket was right about me. How stupid I have been."

And I lay down sobbing in front of the fire. I sobbed so loud and so long that I fell asleep, which, as it turned out, was another very stupid thing to do.

How long I slept I do not know, but when I woke I knew at once that something was wrong. It was my feet—I couldn't feel them!

And that, I discovered to my horror, was because they were *not there*.

I could smell the smoke.

My feet were burnt to ashes.

How was I going to be able to walk without feet?

After that things just went from bad to worse. There was a loud banging on the door, which was then flung open, and into the cottage burst the *Carabiniere*.

"Aha!" he cried. "I've found you, you rascal. Your Mama and Papa have been looking everywhere. You should be ashamed of yourself. I told them, 'He's no good, that one. Make another puppet, Signor Gepetto,' I said. 'This one's nothing but trouble.' And here you are, breaking and entering. Robber! Burglar!"

"My feet," I howled. "I have no feet."

"Good gracious!" said the *Carabiniere*, suddenly much kinder than he had been before. "You poor lad! I have a boy of my own and if he had no feet I'd be dreadfully upset. I shall take you home at once. Don't worry, I'm sure Signor Gepetto will make you some fine new feet. All will be well."

And with that he lifted me up and carried me home singing loud songs all the way to keep me happy. The songs were quite rude in places, but I didn't mind, they made me smile.

Which was why I was smiling in his arms when we met Mama and Papa out in the street, still searching for me high and low. They saw at once what had happened to my feet.

"I'll forget the breaking and entering this time, Signor Gepetto," said the *Carabiniere*, "on account of the fact that he's lost his feet, poor lad."

"And isn't he brave, our little Pinocchio?" said Mama. "Look he's still smiling."

"*Grazie mille*, Signor *Carabiniere*," said Papa, "it was so kind of you to bring our son home to us. He's been a naughty boy, running away like that, but even naughty boys deserve feet. I shall make him some new ones right away."

As I lay there on Papa's workbench having my new feet fitted, Mama gave me a good telling-off, covering me with kisses all the while. But all I could think about was my stomach.

"I'm so hungry, Mama," I whispered. "Can I have

some chocolate?"

"We're not made of money, Pinocchio," Papa said.

"Can I have some bread then?" I asked. "Please?"

"I didn't bake any," said Mama. "How could I? We've been out looking for you day and night. But I do have three pears left."

"I want all of them," I said. "And peeled. I don't like to chew the skin."

As Mama peeled the pears for me, Papa shook his head. "You will spoil this child," he told her, as Mama fed me the first pear.

In fact, I ate all three pears, lickety-split. But I was still hungry.

"Mama," I wailed.

"There's nothing else,

dearest," said Mama. "Just the cores and the skin."

"Well, I'm not eating those," I said, "not in a million years."

"Waste not, want not," said Papa. "If you're really hungry, you'll eat them."

A minute later I'd gobbled down the lot and I wasn't hungry any more. Papa was right.

The Talking Cricket had been right.

I wasn't sure I liked everyone else being quite so right.

Papa sat me up on the workbench and told me to wiggle my feet. They worked!

"What wonderful new feet you have, Pinocchio," said Mama. "I think they are even better than the feet you had before—such elegant, strong feet. Bravo, Papa!"

"Now I have made you new feet, Pinocchio," said Papa, "you will be good, won't you?"

"We don't want you using your lovely new feet to run away with," Mama said, kissing me again and hugging me. "Promise me."

I so loved her hugging me, I would have promised her anything. I leapt down from the workbench and jumped and skipped and danced around the room, trying out my new feet for size. They were perfect.

"I promise!" I cried. "From now on I will be a good boy; I will go to school and never run away again. But Mama, can you make me some clothes for school? The other children, they all tease me. It's bad enough just being a puppet, they say, but a puppet with no clothes, it's embarrassing. They've all got clothes, Mama, and I haven't."

Mama lost no time. She made me a suit out of an old bedspread, and a fine feather hat in bright green, and Papa soon fashioned me some smart leather shoes. I stood in front of them, gave them a twirl, showing myself off proudly.

"What a handsome son we have, Papa," Mama cried, clasping Papa's hand.

"Yes," I said, "but now I need to be smart too. So I need a school book, an ABC, like all the others have."

Mama and Papa looked at me sadly.

"Pinocchio," said Papa, "you have to understand. Mama and me, we can make things with our hands, whatever you like. We are good with our hands. But we are poor people, and books cost money. We just don't have the money; I am sorry."

I could see Papa was near to tears.

After all he has done for me, I thought. *How could I be so thoughtless, so greedy, so selfish!*

"I didn't mean to upset you, Papa," I said. "It's all right, don't worry about it. I can manage without silly old books."

Moments later Papa was putting on his old coat, full of darns and patches like all his clothes. "I won't be long," was all he said, and then he was gone.

Mama took me up on her knee by the fire.

"Your Papa hates to be reminded that we are poor. He does his best. He works hard. He loves us. He is a good man, Pinocchio, the best of men. Be kind to him always.

"Think before you speak," she went on. "Words can hurt, Pinocchio, just as much as sticks and stones."

Papa came back an hour or so later, smiling from ear to ear as he came in the door.

"Here you are, Pinocchio, my boy," he said. "Look what I have for you." He had a book in his hand. "For you, Pinocchio. Your ABC for school."

"Papa?" Mama said. "Where is your coat? What have you done with it?"

"I sold it," Papa said, "to buy the book for the boy. What can be more important to a boy than learning?" He shrugged. "Anyway, that old coat was always too warm for me, too long in the sleeve, and it itched. I'm better off without it."

What a truly wonderful father I had. I ran to him, leapt into his arms and hugged him.

"Papa!" I cried. "How glad I am to have you for a father. I will never let you down. Not in a million years, I promise you!"

CHAPTER THREE

A puppet show and a sneezing Fire Eater

I couldn't have been happier or more excited the next morning, as I said goodbye to Mama and Papa and set off to school in my brand-new clothes with my ABC under my arm. I'd worked it all out.

Today I'll learn to read, just like that, lickety-split.

Tomorrow I'll learn to write. Easy.

The day after tomorrow I'll learn all the arithmetic there is to learn. Simple. Easy as falling off a log.

Then I'll leave school and be able to earn tons

of money, cartloads of it.

Then in a week or so I'll be able to buy Papa a new coat, no patches, with buttons of gold and mother-of-pearl. No one deserves it more after what he's done for me. And I'll buy a fine silk dress for Mama, and diamonds. She shall have all the diamonds she wants. I'll make them so proud of me, and I'll make me proud of me too!

My head was full of all these dreams as I skipped off down the hill toward school. But just then, not far away, I heard the sound of music. It sounded like pipes and drums.

Te-dee, Te-dum, Te-dee, Te-dum, Te-dee, Te-dum.

It echoed through the town.

The trouble was that school was one way and the sound of the band was the other way. I hemmed and hawed, I dallied and dithered. I knew I should really go to school, be a good boy, and that Mama and Papa would be so disappointed if I didn't. But the music was so exciting.

The pipes trilled and the drums pounded and I couldn't seem to help myself—I turned my face away from school. I could do school tomorrow, I thought. Mama and Papa won't know.

And then I ran, *clippety-cloppety, clippety-cloppety*, down the street toward the sound of the band, all thought of school now quite out of my mind.

As I reached the town square I saw a huge tent with a great sign above it, which I couldn't read of course. There were crowds everywhere. The man standing next to me looked like a gentleman who could read. He was dressed in a smart coat and hat, and was carrying a silver-topped cane.

"'Scuse me, sir, but what does that sign say up there?" I asked him.

"It says 'The Greatest Puppet Show in the World.' Just your sort of show, by the look of you," he said, laughing.

"When does it start?"

"Right now. Tickets for sale over there."

"And how much does it cost?"

"Four pennies."

By now wild horses wouldn't have stopped me going in. I could hear the audience clapping and cheering.

"Please, sir," I said, "I haven't got four pennies, but I have got this coat of mine and my hat. You can have my shoes too, if you like."

"What use are they to me?" the gentleman scoffed.

"You're just a little puppet, tiny. Nothing you have would fit me. Besides, as you see, I have a coat and hat and shoes already."

I still can't believe what I said next.

"What about this book of mine, sir?" I said. "It's brand new from the shop yesterday, an ABC book, and it's never even been used."

The gentleman took it from me and looked through it.

"Very well," he said at last. "My little boy will soon need a book just like this for school. It's a deal." And he gave me four pence. I looked down at the coins in my hand and felt so ashamed of what I had done.

But shame, I discovered, soon passes. The music

was thumping away, the crowds were roaring inside the tent. I ran in, straight to the front row, and sat down.

And what a show it was! Punch and Judy were up there on stage hammering merry heck out of each other. *Biff! Bop! Biff! Bop! Ouch! Aiee! Ow! Biff! Bop!*

Like everyone else in the audience I was howling with laughter at their insults and antics. But then quite suddenly Punch stopped, and Judy stopped. They were both looking straight at me. "A puppet!" they cried. "There's a puppet out there in the audience. Up on to the stage with you! Come on, brother!

Up you come! You belong up here in the limelight where everyone can see you."

I was over the moon. Imagine, me, on the stage! The whole audience began chanting for me. So up I went: with one bound I leapt on to the conductor's head, then the trombonist's, then the drummer's, and there I was in the glare of the lights. A star!

But not for long, as you shall see.

All the puppet players, Punch and Judy too, had stopped their act to greet me. They hugged me and slapped my back. They wanted to know who I was and where I had acted before.

"I'm Pinocchio," I told them, "and I have never been on stage before in my life."

"Then join us, brother Pinocchio. We are the greatest

puppet show in the world. You can be one of us, travel the world with us." And I found myself hoisted on to their shoulders and carried in triumph around the stage.

Meanwhile the audience had grown tired of all this. They began whistling and booing. "The show," they yelled. "Get on with the show! No more of this mucking around. We haven't come to see this. Get on or get off!"

But Punch and Judy and the others were far too busy celebrating the arrival of their new friend to be bothered about the audience any more. Until, that was, this ogre of a man appeared from out of the wings. I didn't like the look of him at all. He was a dastardly looking fellow with a long black beard,

teeth like yellow fangs, eyes that glowed like burning coals, hairy hands, and nails as long and sharp as bear's claws.

"Watch out, Pinocchio," the puppets whispered. "He's the Fire Eater. He can be every bit as nasty as he looks."

"You!" he roared. He had the voice of an ogre too, and his breath smelled of rotten fish.

Like all the other puppets, I was so transfixed with fear that I couldn't move, I couldn't run. So it was all too easy for him to snatch me up. He held me close to his mouth, close enough to see the wobbly red bit at the base of his throat.

"You, puppet, you look as if you are made of well-seasoned wood—cherry-wood, I'd say. Yes, you'll burn very nicely indeed; just what I need for my cooking fire. I have a fine fat lamb turning on the spit right now. If I throw you on the fire, you'll finish the roasting off perfectly."

I was wiggling like an eel and screeching like an owl. "Please, sir. I have only just been born, sir, and I don't want to die. Please, sir, Mr. Fire Eater. Be kind, be merciful, I beg you. I'm a good puppet, I can do anything."

But the Fire Eater shook his head. "Into the fire with you. I've got quite enough puppets as it is."

If my newfound puppet friends hadn't come to my aid at that very moment I should have ended up in the fire, and that would have been the end of my story.

Punch and Judy, frightened though they were of this ogre of a man, begged him and begged him.

"Burn us instead!" they cried. "Pinocchio is only young. You could train him up, signor, teach him tricks. He's strong, he's smart, he'll learn. He can be the star of the show."

I could feel the flames on my back by now, I was that close to the fire.

"Please, signor, they'll come for miles around to see Pinocchio," said Punch.

"Please, signor, you'll make lots of money," cried Judy. "They don't want to see just any old Punch and Judy show. Pinocchio is a new kind of puppet, a boy puppet, unique, the only one like it in the whole world."

At that the Fire Eater paused and looked down at me, examining me closely.

"Mmm, maybe you're right," he said. "Maybe."

And then he sneezed, loudly, violently, again and again. I was terrified. I thought at any moment he might drop me on the fire.

"A good sign," Punch whispered to me. "He only sneezes when he's feeling kind. Say 'Bless you, signor.' It'll make him feel even kinder toward you."

"Bless you, signor," I said, again and again, every time he sneezed.

As he finished sneezing a beaming smile came over his face so that suddenly he seemed not

nearly so ugly as before. "Very well," he said. "I can see you are a kind and polite boy. And in any case you are a bit thin and spindly for the fire, so I shall spare you. But somehow or other my lamb must be cooked. I'll have to burn you two instead."

And with that he dropped me and snatched up Punch and Judy.

After what they had just done for me, I didn't hesitate. I fell on my knees in front of the Fire Eater and pleaded with him.

"Please, kind sir, please, gentle signor, please, merciful master. Don't harm them. They are my friends. Have pity, signor."

"I am hungry, and I like my lamb well cooked," he replied, kicking me aside with his boot. "Out of my way."

I tumbled over and found myself sitting between

the spit and the Fire Eater. I leapt to my feet and held out my arms. "Then I shall die with them in the flames, sir, so that you can have your lamb well cooked. Tie me up and throw me in with them."

What had come over me?

Here I was, on the spur of the moment, offering to sacrifice my life for friendship. I'd never before done anything brave or even said anything brave.

To my great relief, I saw the Fire Eater's face softening. He was smiling down at me again.

"What a kind and courageous little boy you are, Pinocchio. Any man would be proud to have such a brave son as you. I shall have my lamb pink today, half cooked—it's very good that way anyway, I'm told. And I shall burn no puppets. Off you go with your friends, Pinocchio—have fun!"

And that's just what we did. On the stage that night we held a puppet party, singing and dancing all night long, and I was the hero of the hour. I liked being liked, I liked being a hero. In fact I liked it so much that when

the Fire Eater asked me to join the troupe of puppets and to learn to act and dance and sing alongside my puppet friends, I was giddy with joy.

But then, after a few weeks had gone by, I began to feel homesick. Though I was happy enough among my new friends, I could not put it out of my mind just how mean I had been to Papa. He'd sold the coat off his back to buy me my ABC book. And what had I done with it?

I could hardly sleep at night for thinking about Mama and Papa, how badly I had treated them, how sad they would both be without me. I missed them more and more each day and at last made up my mind to confess my whole story to the Fire Eater and my puppet friends.

As they listened, the Fire Eater wept buckets and sneezed repeatedly.

When I'd finished, it was he who spoke up. "We have all come to love you like our own, little Pinocchio," he sniffled. "Of course, we understand you must go home where you belong. So take these five gold coins with you for your poor Papa and Mama—they have greater need of money than I."

So the very next morning, after fond and tearful farewells from the puppets, and a bear hug from the Fire Eater that squeezed me half to death, I set off toward home, the gold coins jingling in my pocket. I was sad in a way to leave, but at the same time happier than I had ever been in all my life, because I knew I was going home to Mama and Papa to say sorry, to ask for their forgiveness. For a change I was doing the right thing.

CHAPTER FOUR

Five gold coins and a strange meeting with a lame fox and a blind cat

So there I was on my way home down a long forest road, whistling cheerily, longing to see my home again, longing to give my precious five coins to Papa in repayment for his coat, when I saw a fox and a cat coming toward me.

They were a strange looking pair. The fox was limping, and leaning heavily on the arm of the cat, but at the same time he seemed to be leading the cat, who was quite obviously blind.

Things became stranger still when we got talking. They could not have been more friendly and polite. But what puzzled me at once was how they greeted me.

"Good day, Master Pinocchio," said the Lame Fox.

"Good day, Master Pinocchio," said the Blind Cat.

As you will see, they repeated one another rather often.

"How do you know my name?" I asked them.

"Well, we know your dear Papa and Mama. Everyone knows how they've been looking for their dear little puppet son. All day and every day. And now we've found you. There's no one else who looks quite like you, Pinocchio, you know."

"How is my Papa?" I asked. "How is my Mama?"

"Well, we have to be quite honest," replied the Lame Fox.

"Quite honest," echoed the Blind Cat.

"He was looking rather pinched up and cold without his coat, and your Mama was beside herself with sadness."

"They won't have to be sad any more," I told them, "not when they see what I have for them."

"What do you have?" said the Lame Fox.

"Do you have?" echoed the Blind Cat.

I took the coins out of my pocket and showed them proudly.

"Gold, real gold coins!" I cried. "I'm rich! I can buy Gepetto a handsome new coat, real velvet if he wants, mother-of-pearl buttons, and Mama will never have to go hungry again as long as she lives. And I will buy myself a new ABC book, and go back to school, and make Papa and Mama proud of me."

"Very wise, dear boy," said the Lame Fox, suddenly

limping particularly heavily.

"Very wise," echoed the Blind Cat, stumbling particularly clumsily.

The Lame Fox continued. "If we'd studied hard at school, we wouldn't have ended up like this: a couple of poor old crocks with one good pair of eyes and one good pair of legs between us. You are right, dear boy, school's the thing!"

"School's the thing," echoed the Blind Cat.

Just then a blackbird called out from a bush nearby. "Look out, Pinocchio, things are not always what they seem. These two tricksters—"

But the blackbird never finished speaking, for in a flash the Blind Cat leapt on him, and tore him to bits. All that was left was a scattering of feathers.

"Why did you do that?" cried Pinocchio when

he'd gotten over the shock.

"I was teaching him a lesson," said the Blind Cat, licking his lips. "He was far too chatty."

"You shouldn't have," I said. "Poor blackbird."

"Don't worry, Pinocchio, dear boy," said the Lame Fox. "We have more important things than blackbirds to tell you about."

"Tell you about," said the Blind Cat, still licking his lips.

Something was bothering me. I had to ask.

"'Scuse me," I said, "but if you're blind, how could you leap up on a blackbird like that and kill it?"

"I go for the sound," answered the Blind Cat. "Kill the song, you kill the bird. It's an old saying of mine."

"Now," the Lame Fox went on, "Pinocchio, dear boy, about those five gold pieces…"

"Five gold pieces," said the Blind Cat.

"What if I told you that we know a way to turn your five miserable coins into a treasure trove of gold coins, hundreds of them, thousands, tens of thousands. What would you think of that?"

"Is it magic or something?" I asked.

"No, dear boy, no, no," the Lame Fox replied. "Nothing so crude. All you have to do is to come with us to a field near the City of Simple Simons—you may have heard of it. Everyone there is stinking rich."

"But how did they get rich in the first place?" I asked. "What do they do?"

"Well I'll tell you. Alongside this field, there's this very special hedge…." said the Lame Fox.

"Hedge," said the Blind Cat.

"And the field is called the Field of Wonders."

"Wonders," said the Blind Cat.

"All we do…they do…you do, is bury your coins under the hedge in this field, sprinkle the place with a little water—very important is water. Then we all go to bed. And in the morning your five coins will have become a fortune in gold—a huge, humongous treasure of gold coins. Overnight, your coins will have grown like little acorns in the soil into a great tree that will blossom. And not pink blossoms, dear boy, not white blossoms, but gold blossoms, glittering in the sun. And we can pick them all and be rich. We—I mean, you—can pick them all and be rich as Croesus forever, your Mama and Papa too. Signor Gepetto will never have to work again; Signora Gepetto will never have to cook again. What a life for you it will be!"

"What a life!" said the Blind Cat.

I know what you're thinking. You're thinking, Don't do it, Pinocchio! Don't be a wooden-head again. Don't believe them! Well, I'm sorry to say I believed what I wanted to believe; I fell for it hook, line and sinker. When I look back on it now, I can't believe how stupid I was.

I danced with joy. "How wonderful!" I cried. "And you can have some of the golden blossoms too."

"No, no, no," the Lame Fox said, shaking his head. "We couldn't accept. We're doing this just for you, Pinocchio, for you and for your poor Mama and Papa."

"Poor Mama and Papa," said the Blind Cat.

And off we went at once down the dark, empty road toward the glittering lights in the distance.

"Those lights, they look like gold," I said.

"They are gold, dear boy," said the Lame Fox. "That's the City of Simple Simons. Everything glitters in the City of Simple Simons because everything is made of gold."

"Gold," said the Blind Cat.

CHAPTER FIVE

At the Inn of the Red Lobster, and that Talking Cricket again (yes, I know you thought he was dead, and so did I!)

We walked and walked, but the twinkly lights of the City of Simple Simons never seemed to get any closer. As the evening came on we found ourselves walking through a small village, all of us tired out. It was the Lame Fox who suggested we stop the night at the village inn, the Inn of the Red Lobster.

"We can have just a little nibble to eat, have a good

night's sleep and then we'll be on our way again, toward the City of Simple Simons and the Field of Wonders."

It seemed like a good idea to me. We all sat down to eat in front of the fire, and soon enough, in came the food.

"Only a nibble, you understand," said the Lame Fox. "I don't eat much. I'm on a diet, doctor's orders, only a nibble." But all the same he managed to wolf down a whole hare, some partridges, a few pheasants, a couple of rabbits, and half a dozen frogs and lizards. That was all.

"Only a nibble, I don't eat much either. I'm not feeling well," said the Blind Cat, who then proceeded to eat his way through thirty-five meatballs in tomato sauce, then gobbled up four helpings of tripe in cheese sauce.

Just watching them ruined my appetite. I was so

excited all I could manage was a few nuts and a crust of bread.

I couldn't get to sleep for a long while that night. All I could think about was the Field of Wonders and the gold that would soon be mine. By this time tomorrow I'd be rich, rich, rich!

But I did fall asleep in the end, and when I did, I dreamed.

I dreamed I was walking through fields of golden corn, and all around the trees grew golden leaves, even the clouds in the sky were gold.

I was awoken in the morning by a loud knocking at my door.

"Time to get up, Pinocchio, lazy head," the Inn Keeper bellowed. "Your friends are up already and gone two hours ago. They wanted me to say goodbye for them. The Blind Cat had news his son was dying—chilblains, I think he said. Oh yes, and by the way, they said that you wouldn't mind paying the bill."

Actually I did mind, but I couldn't say so, could I?

I went downstairs and paid the bill. I was not a happy puppet, I can tell you, as I handed over one of my fine gold coins.

"Your friends said they'd meet you at the Field of Wonders," said the Inn Keeper. "Go to the City of Simple Simons as soon as you can, they said. Someone will tell you the way."

So off I went on my own.

"What's one gold coin?" I asked myself, counting the four I had left. "When I get to the Field of Wonders and plant the others, I'll have hundreds of gold pieces, thousands. And to have a son die of chilblains must be terrible."

And I know what you must be thinking. How could
you be that gullible, that stupid, Pinocchio? I've been
asking myself that question off and on ever since. I
mean, why is it that I so often believed what I wanted
to believe. Why didn't I think? Silly me! Silly, silly me!

The road took me into a dark forest.

All around me I heard rustlings and snortings. I
could feel eyes watching me.

I whistled as loudly as I could to show how brave I
was. But I wasn't. I was terrified.

The noises were coming closer, louder. There were
bears and wolves in these woods, and they were after me.

"Don't worry, Pinocchio," came a little voice.

I looked up and saw on a nearby tree trunk a tiny glowing light. I went closer to see what it was.

It spoke again. "I am the ghost of Talking Cricket— the one you killed, remember?"

"Go away," I cried, not wanting to be reminded of the terrible murder I had committed.

"You know exactly what you should do, Pinocchio, don't you? Go home to poor Gepetto and his wife. Go home to your Mama and Papa. They cry for you day and night."

"It's none of your business, Talking Cricket," I said. "Anyway, I will go home when I've made my fortune in gold, and not before. These four gold coins will become thousands, and my Mama and Papa will have riches beyond their wildest dreams."

"You silly puppet. Money doesn't grow on trees.

You have to earn it. Anyone who tells you different is either a fool or a swindler. Go home. You're a good boy at heart, Pinocchio, I know you are. For goodness' sake, do what your heart tells you is right."

"What do you know? You're just a Talking Cricket," I shouted at him. "In fact you're not even that, you're just the ghost of a Talking Cricket. Why should I listen to you?"

"Because I am your conscience, Pinocchio. The little voice in your head that will always remind you of what is right and what is wrong."

"I'll do what I want to do," I yelled at him. "Go away. Or I'll kill you again!"

"Please yourself, Pinocchio, but watch out for the

thieves and robbers and bandits, that's all I can say. There're a lot of them about, behind every bush, every tree."

"Get lost, Talking Cricket," I shouted. "I don't believe in ghosts. I don't. You're not real. You're only a ghost and I don't believe in ghosts. I don't. I don't."

And at once the light went out and I was alone again in the dark of the forest. I hurried on.

Robbers, thieves, bandits. Am I frightened of them? No! I told myself. Then I shouted it aloud to drown out the sounds of all the stirrings in the forest. "I'm not scared of you. I'm Pinocchio. I'm not scared of tigers, of wolves, even of stupid Talking Cricket ghosts."

But I'd only got a little farther when two shadowy cloaked figures emerged from the trees in front of me,

one shorter than the other, both of them wearing masks.

The Talking Cricket had been right! I knew at once they must be bandits and I knew what they would be after, too. My gold coins!

Before they got to me, I put the coins into my mouth and held them under my tongue.

"Your money or your life, puppet!" they cried, holding a dagger at my throat. There was something about the way they spoke that I recognized, but I couldn't think what it was.

Maybe you can.

I couldn't reply, of course. My gold coins would clink inside my mouth if I tried to speak.

"Come on, dear boy," said the shorter one, "give us your gold, or you're a dead man, a dead puppet."

"Dead puppet," echoed the other bandit.

"And when we've killed you," the short one went on, pressing the dagger under my throat, "we'll go and kill your Papa and your Mama too."

"Mama too," snarled the other.

"Oh, please don't," I cried. "Please don't harm them."

And as soon as I said it the coins clinked in my mouth so that they knew exactly where they were. They went crazy. They grabbed me by my nose and tried to pry open my mouth with the dagger.

I knew that I was fighting for my life, for Mama and Papa's lives too, and all fear suddenly left me. I kicked and bit and scratched. I fought like a wild thing. I might only have been a spindly little puppet, but when I was angry I was strong.

I managed to escape from their clutches and bolted. I dashed through the trees until I came to open fields. I could hear them close behind me, cursing me, and telling me all the terrible things they were going to do when they caught up with me.

For a while I ran even faster, leaping over ditches and streams. But it was no good. They were gaining on me all the time, and all the time my legs were weakening. So when I came to a tall pine tree, I didn't

think twice. I was up it in a flash, lickety-split, climbing to the topmost branches.

I sat up there and got my breath back. At first they tried to climb up after me—but I was relieved to see that they couldn't manage it. I thumbed my nose at them, and called them all the rude names I could think of—well, I thought I was safe, didn't I?

But it wasn't long before they

came up with a different plan. They began to drag branches from all around to build a fire, right around the foot of the tree. They were going to burn me out. I prayed the fire wouldn't catch. But it did, and quickly, all too quickly. Soon the flames were roaring up from below and the whole tree began to crackle and smoke.

It was the smoke in the end that saved me. Holding my breath, under cover of the smoke, I shimmied down the tree and sprang to the ground. Off I went again, running as fast as my legs would carry me, knowing that as soon as I came out of the smoke they would see me again and give chase.

I was some way ahead of them when I came to a river, fast flowing and muddy. I reckoned it might be possible to jump it if I judged it just right, if I was lucky. I had little choice anyway, didn't I?

So I went for it.

I'd never leapt so high or so far in all my life.

I was over!

From the other side, I turned to watch those two villainous bandits, as they prepared to make the jump themselves.

Joy, oh joy, they landed right in the river, right up to their necks. I thought they might have drowned. But only moments later, dripping and muddied, I saw them wading toward the bank, and soon they were out and after me again.

So I ran into the tall, dark forest. But the more I ran, the more weak and spindly I felt. Every time I looked around they were closer and closer.

I was sobbing as I ran. When they caught me, they'd cut my throat!

Why hadn't I listened to the ghost of Talking Cricket?

Why? How could I have been so stupid?

My head was spinning. I knew I couldn't go on much longer.

Then suddenly there in front of me I saw the whitewashed walls of a little cottage, bright and welcoming through the trees. If only I could get there before they caught me, I could lock myself in. I could be safe.

I found new strength in my legs, and raced on ahead. I was on my last legs as I reached the cottage and hammered at the door. Above me, an upstairs window opened. I looked up to see the face of a young girl looking down at me. She was beautiful, her hair as blue as the sea, her face as white as wax.

"No one lives here," she said in a deathly whisper.

"No one living anyway, only me."

"I don't care," I cried. "Open the door, please, I beg you. Help me. There are two bandits after me…."

But before I could finish speaking, the pair were on me, dragging me away back into the forest. I was done for. They kicked and beat me, sat on me until I squealed, shook me until I rattled, cursing and yelling at me to open my mouth. But I wouldn't. They could kill me if they wanted, but I would never give up my four gold coins! Never! Never!

"I've got an idea! Let's hang him by the thumbs," said one.

"By the thumbs," said the other.

They grabbed me, and dragged me to a tree. There, despite all my kicking and struggling, they tied a noose around each of my thumbs, threw a rope over a branch

and hauled me up from the ground. I hung there for hour after hour, all hope of rescue gone, but keeping my mouth firmly shut. I would never give in. They would never have my golden coins. I would rather die with them inside my mouth.

After a while the two masked bandits got bored with waiting.

"We'll be back in the morning," said the shorter

bandit as they walked off, "when you're dead."

"Dead," echoed the other one.

"Once you're dead your mouth will be sure to open wide."

"Open wide," echoed the other.

With that they left me swinging and swaying in the wind, waiting to die, the nooses tighter and tighter around my thumbs. My eyes went dim. My head filled up with the silence of death. I knew I couldn't last much longer.

All I could think of was Mama and Papa, and how stupid I'd been. How I would love to see them once more to tell them how sorry I was. How I would miss them when I was dead. I closed my eyes, drifting into sleep, the sleep that would last forever.

CHAPTER SIX

A good fairy, taking my medicine and nose trouble

Inever expected to wake up again. When I did, I wasn't sure whether I was in this world or the next.

I opened my eyes to see a huge falcon hovering right above me, his wings beating the air. I thought he was going to dive down and peck me, but when I looked up into his bright eye, I saw that he was kind and I knew he would not hurt me. Closer and closer to me he hovered, and then, with his powerful beak he began to tear apart the rope that held me by the thumbs.

In a moment I was free, and I felt his claws pinch my shoulders as he gripped hold of me and flew me down over the forest floor, landing me gently on the mossy ground. Then with a great cry of farewell he lifted into the air and flew off.

He had saved me.

For some moments I lay there half dead, half alive, still quite unable to move. I must have fallen unconscious for a while because when I opened my eyes I saw not a falcon, but a white poodle standing over me.

And not any old white poodle. This one wore a tricorn hat and a wig of white curls. He was dressed in a brown velvet coat with sparkly buttons and breeches of crimson velvet, with silk stockings and silver-buckled shoes. I can tell you he was the most overdressed poodle there ever was.

"My name, good sir, is Medoro," he said. "My mistress sent the falcon to rescue you, and she has sent me to bring you home. I have a carriage waiting for you, sir."

And sure enough there, waiting on the road, was an elegant little coach, that looked as if it was made entirely of glass, and drawn, not by a horse, but by a hundred white mice.

The poodle helped me up into the carriage and laid me gently down on deep, feathery cushions. Then he got up into the driver's seat; and with a click of the poodle's tongue, off the mice trotted, the ride so smooth that I hardly felt it.

I was still not sure if all this was not just a wonderful dream.

When the coach stopped I saw that we had pulled up at the same little white cottage I'd been to before in the forest; and outside it stood the same lovely girl with the same blue hair and waxen skin, more fairy than human. It was she who carried me upstairs into a sweet bedroom where all the walls were mother-of-pearl, and sat by my bed stroking my forehead and singing to me softly. I thought then that I had truly died and gone to heaven.

"I have sent for the doctors, little one," she said. "They are the best and nicest doctors I know. They will examine you and make you well again. One is a cackling crow, one is a hooting owl, and the last is a dear friend of mine, a talking cricket."

The Talking Cricket! Not him!

How ashamed of myself I felt. I didn't want to have

to face him again, not after what I'd done. Hadn't he warned me again and again?

And I still had my gold coins hidden under my tongue. How was I going to explain them away? I didn't want those doctors to discover them.

Keep quiet, I told myself. *Just keep quiet. Don't open your mouth. Don't say a word. Pretend to be asleep.*

By the time they arrived I was pretending to be in such a deep sleep, the crow and the owl couldn't make up their minds whether I was alive or dead. They prodded and pecked me, tapped my knees, listened to my heart. I didn't move. Then the Talking Cricket spoke up.

"Just a moment, I think I know this puppet," he said. "Yes, I do! Dead or alive, he is a headstrong rascal who never takes advice. He's a runaway who's breaking his Mama's heart and making his Papa's life a misery."

I couldn't help myself then. The Talking Cricket was so right. I started to sob and sob, my whole body shaking.

"Well, I see he's not dead after all. I've cured him," declared the Hooting Owl.

"I was the one to cure him," boasted the Cackling Crow.

"I think you'll find it was me," said the Talking Cricket.

"Maybe this is a good sign, though. This puppet, even if he's half dead, still has some shame. He could make something of himself after all, if he lives."

When I opened my eyes the doctors were gone, and only the Good Fairy remained. She bent over and kissed me tenderly on the forehead.

"Sweet dreams, Pinocchio," she said, and with that she left the room.

At once I took out the four gold coins and hid them under my pillow. I fell asleep completely this time, but my dreams were very far from sweet. In my feverish sleep I tossed and turned, and when I dreamed, I dreamed of the Good Fairy. She was bending over me, lifting my head, trying to get me to drink some medicine from a glass.

"Drink it, Pinocchio, dearest, please. It'll make you better."

"Shan't," I said. "Don't like medicine. It's too bitter."

"I'll give you a lump of sugar afterwards to take away the taste."

"I want the sugar first," I told her. "Now!"

"You promise you'll take the medicine after, like a good boy?"

"Yes," I said.

The sugar lump was delicious.

Then she tried again to make me take the medicine.

"Shan't," I said, clamping my lips shut.

"Pinocchio, dearest, please," she begged me. "You're a very sick boy, you know. You have a bad fever, and if you don't take this medicine, it will only get worse, and if a fever gets worse and worse... well, you might even die."

"Don't care. That medicine's horrible. I can smell it. I'd rather die than drink it."

"Very well, Pinocchio," she said. "I don't like to do this. But I have to, for your own good."

The moment she said it, the door flew open and in came four rabbits, black as coal. They walked solemnly toward me, carrying on their shoulders a small black coffin.

"Who's that for?" I asked in fear, and trembling.

"For you, dear Pinocchio," said the fairy.

"But I'm not dead," I cried.

"You soon will be," said the fairy, "if you don't take your medicine."

"Oh no, no, no," I wailed. "I don't want to die. I'll take the medicine, I will. Give it to me."

I took the glass in my hands and swallowed every last drop. At once I felt better and I sprang out of bed. "You see," I cried, "I'm not dead. My legs work, my arms work. I'm alive, I'm alive!"

The four black rabbits did not look at all happy to see me so hale and hearty, but I didn't care about them. I was so glad not to be dead I threw my arms around the Good Fairy. "Thank you, thank you, dear, sweet fairy," I said.

"Now I must feed you up and make you strong again, Pinocchio, dear."

Then she sat me down in front of the fire and fed me a bowl of piping hot leek and potato soup. Soon I was feeling much better.

I talked and talked, telling the good, kind fairy all my adventures, about the bandits who had jumped me, how I'd hidden the golden coins in my mouth, and how they had hung me from a tree so that my mouth would fall open and the coins would fall out.

"Where are those coins now, Pinocchio, dear?" asked the fairy.

She's after them too! I thought at once. Even the Good Fairy may not be as good as she seems. *Everyone's after my gold coins!*

So I lied. "Er... I lost them, in the forest," I told her.

Suddenly I felt my nose twitching, stretching itself. It was growing longer!

"Anything that's lost can be found," said the fairy. "Tell me where you lost them and we can go and look for them."

Er...oh yes...I remember now," I said. I didn't lose them, I swallowed them when I took the medicine."

My nose was growing longer still, as long as a cucumber. I turned away to hide my face so she couldn't see.

By now my nose was so long it touched the window pane.

The Good Fairy was laughing.

"Your nose, Pinocchio, your nose! If you lie any more it will grow so long you won't be able to get out of the door."

I was filled with shame at having been caught out. I couldn't look her in the face. I just wanted to run away and hide myself.

I ran for the door, but I couldn't get close enough to open it. My nose was too long. She was right, like the Talking Cricket had been, right about everything.

A moment later she clapped her hands. Hundreds of red woodpeckers seemed to fill the room, all of them settling on my nose and pecking at it furiously, until my head was filled with the thunder of their knocking.

I'd have no nose left!

That's what must have woken me from my dream, those woodpeckers. I woke up crying my heart out. At once I felt my nose to see if any of it was still there. How relieved I was that the horrid woodpeckers hadn't pecked it all away. But still, I couldn't stop crying.

The Good Fairy came to me and put her arms around me.

"I had such a terrible nightmare," I told her.

"No, it wasn't a nightmare, dear Pinocchio," she

said. "It happened, all of it. The medicine, the black rabbits… But don't worry, it's all over now. I shall be like a good sister to you, and look after you. You can stay here with me as long as you like. We shall look after one another. Would you like that? You can call me sister dear, and I shall call you brother dear. And we shall be family."

"I should love to stay, sister dear, but what about Mama and Papa?" I said. "They'll be worrying themselves sick about me."

"Don't worry, brother dear, I have taken care of that. I have sent for them already. They are on the road right now, on their way."

"That's wonderful," I cried, "I shall run and meet them."

I got myself dressed right away and when she

wasn't looking I took the gold coins out from under the pillow and stuffed them in my trouser pocket. Then, kissing my newfound sister goodbye, I ran out of the house and off down the road.

I hadn't gone that far. I was skipping along quite happily when who should I meet coming toward me but the Lame Fox and the Blind Cat.

"We've been looking for you everywhere, Pinocchio!" they cried. "Where did you go? What happened to you?"

I told them the whole story, all about the horrible bandits. I still didn't realize who the bandits had been. *Yes, I was that stupid! Stupid, stupid, stupid!*

And of course I told them about my Good Fairy, my dear sister who had looked after me and cared for me.

"Fairies, bandits, ahem, you have had an exciting time!" said the Lame Fox.

"Exciting time," echoed the Blind Cat.

"And, if you don't mind my asking, ahem," coughed the Lame Fox, "what about your gold pieces? Do you, ahem, still have them, ahem?"

"Ahem!" coughed the Blind Cat.

"Got them," I told them, patting my trouser pocket, "safely here."

"Well then, let's go to the Field of Wonders right away, Pinocchio," wheezed the Lame Fox, putting an arm around me. "All we have to do is to plant your four gold coins in the earth and an hour or two later, four will become two thousand, three, four, five thousand. Depending, of course, on how fast the tree of gold blossoms."

"Five thousand coins," I breathed. "That many, really? Are you sure?"

"Oh, quite sure, ahem," said the Lame Fox. "It's only a couple of miles or so down this road, my dear."

"But I've just remembered," I told them, "I have to meet my Mama and Papa. They're coming to find me."

"A little lesson in life, Pinocchio," whispered the

Lame Fox confidentially into my ear. "If a thing's worth doing, it's worth doing now. Later may be too late. Think of it: five thousand gold coins."

"Five thousand gold coins," the Blind Cat whispered in my other ear.

Well, I ask you, how could I refuse? Don't be too quick to blame me. I mean, what would you have done? Be honest now! I'm not proud of myself, not at all. I'm ashamed to say, I quickly forgot all about dear Mama and Papa and I went along with them quite happily.

We had to walk right through the City of Simple Simons to get to the Field of Wonders. That was a sad and strange place, I can tell you.

Everyone was wandering around like ragged ghosts,

hollow-cheeked and pale and hungry. Every dog I saw was hairless, all the sheep were shaved of their wool and trembling with cold. The butterflies had no color in their wings and couldn't fly. Peacocks and pheasants had lost their tails and all their bright feathers. It was a place where everyone and everything was so sad. I couldn't understand why.

And then, just outside the walls of this city of sadness, we followed a stream to a small field, much like any other.

"Here we are," said the Lame Fox. "The earth looks fine, just here. You dig the hole, Pinocchio."

So I did as he told me, with the Lame Fox and the Blind Cat looking over my shoulder. I planted my gold coins, and covered them up with earth.

"Now," said the Lame Fox, "go down to the stream, fill your shoes with water, Pinocchio, and sprinkle it on the earth. And in an hour or two, believe you us…"

"Believe you us," echoed the Blind Cat.

"…your tree," continued the Lame Fox, "will be standing there in full leaf, in full, golden blossom."

"In full golden blossom," whispered the Blind Cat.

They turned to go.

"And now we must be on our way. We have done our good deed and made you the richest puppet in the whole country, in the whole world probably. What more could you ask?"

I thanked them from the bottom of my heart, tried to persuade them to stay, to let me give them at least some of the gold as a reward for their kindness and generosity. They wouldn't hear of it.

So I waved goodbye to them and walked down to the stream to fetch water in my shoes, just as they'd told me. I came back and sprinkled the water on the earth and then crouched down to wait for the first shoots of my tree of golden blossoms to show.

I waited, and I waited, and I waited.

Hour after hour I crouched there.

Nothing happened.

Nothing grew.

CHAPTER SEVEN

In prison and in the doghouse

"**T**his tree is taking a very long time to grow," I said to myself. "But it'll be worth the wait. Imagine, Pinocchio, five thousand golden coins, maybe more. I'm going to build a great marble palace with my treasure, stables full of horses, cellars full of lemonade, and a library too, but not filled with boring old books—no!—a library of cakes and candy and cookies."

Still I crouched there.

Still I dreamed my dreams of the good life and endless riches.

But did I see anything grow in this patch of earth? Not a thing.

In the end I dropped off to sleep.

Psst! I heard half in my dreams. "Psst!"

I opened my eyes. It was a wiggly worm.

"Psst! Wake up, little puppety thing. Wake up!" He was shaking his head sadly. "Who's a silly boy, then?" he whispered—worms can only whisper, if you didn't know.

I felt like stamping on him and squashing him, but a little voice in my head stopped me, a voice I recognized only too well. *Don't do it,* the Talking Cricket was telling me. And for once, I took his advice.

The next moment I heard a great screeching. I looked up. A big red and green squawking parrot was circling above my head, mocking me, laughing at me. I was so angry. I bent down and picked up a clod of earth and hurled it at him.

"Who's a silly boy, then?" he squawked.

"What are you laughing at?" I cried. "Go away!"

"I'm laughing because you are such a dumbo, Pinocchio," he said. "Do you really think your four gold pieces could grow into five thousand, just like that?"

"What world were you born into?" whispered the Wiggly Worm. "Maybe you just believe what you want to believe. Have a look in the hole you dug, Pinocchio. I saw it all with my own eyes. While you were asleep, the Lame Fox and the Blind Cat dug up your gold coins. They're long gone by now."

"He's right," said the Squawking Parrot. "You've lost it all, and all because you're so greedy, you dumbo."

I clawed frantically in the earth. They were both right. The gold was gone.

"You see?" cried the Squawking Parrot. "What did I tell you?"

In my fury I hurled more handfuls of earth at him.

"No use being angry with him, Pinocchio," whispered the Wiggly Worm. "Be angry with yourself."

But it was the Lame Fox and the Blind Cat who I was angry with. I wanted revenge on those two cheats. I wanted them to be punished. I ran back into the City of Simple Simons and went straight to the Court House and reported the robbery to the Judge.

I know this next part is difficult to believe, but you've believed the rest (well, I hope you have because it's all true, every word)!

The Judge turned out to be a frowning gorilla. He was a silverback with wise brown eyes. As he listened to my tale of woe, how I'd been tricked by the Lame Fox and the Blind Cat and how they'd gone off with my gold coins, his eyes narrowed and I could see he, like me, was becoming more annoyed and upset at my tale.

"Please, your wonderfulness," I pleaded. "I want them to be caught, chained up and put in prison for a very long time, with nothing but bread and water."

The Frowning Gorilla held up his hand and pronounced his verdict. "Prison it will be. Bread and water it will be. But not for them. For you!" he cried, pointing at me. "For your sheer stupidity and greediness, you will go to prison for ten years. Take him away."

I could not believe it.

For all the long, long months as I languished in jail I still could not believe it. I had plenty of time in my dark, dark cell to think about how stupid and silly and greedy I had been.

The Wiggly Worm was right, the Squawking Parrot was right, the Talking Cricket was right. The Good Fairy too. When would I ever learn?

Everyone I loved I had let down, myself most of all.

I howled myself to sleep every night, and longed for my beloved Mama and Papa, and my Good Fairy, my dear, sweet sister. Every day seemed like a year. The bread was full of maggots and the water was green with slime.

I knew I had to escape somehow, or I would die, but it took me a while to figure out my plan. It was a good plan, I thought, but would it work?

One morning when my jailer came in, I pretended to be dead. I lay there, my eyes wide open, stiff as wood—which was not difficult for me.

He shouted at me to wake up.

I didn't.

He shook me. I rattled, but still I played dead.

"This is a very dead puppet," he said, prodding me. "No need to waste any more of our best bread and water on this one."

My plan was working! He picked me up by my neck and threw me out of the back door of the prison. I landed in a stinking pile of rubbish, but didn't move until I was quite sure he'd gone back inside. Then I got up and ran. I ran, like I'd never run before.

I made straight for the Good Fairy's cottage. Soon I would see my dear sister. She'd have food for me and

I was so hungry; she would look after me. And maybe my Mama and Papa would be there too, and we'd all be together, one happy family, and I'd eat cakes and drink lemonade, and everything would be wonderful again—particularly the part about cakes and lemonade. That thought kept me going as I ran down the muddy road homewards.

All the while as I ran, I promised myself out loud never ever again to be so stupid and selfish and greedy.

"Always remember, Pinocchio," I told myself, "what a complete fool you have been. Always remember that empty hole in the ground, always remember those long months in prison, and maggoty bread and the slimy green water. Never forget."

I must have been almost there when I was stopped in my tracks by the strangest, most terrifying sight. On the path ahead of me there was a snake, but not just any old snake. It was a huge dragony kind, with bright green scales and fiery red eyes that glared. There were flames coming out of his mouth, and his tail was smoking like a chimney.

I wasn't going to risk trying to get past him, so I asked him nervously, but very politely, if he would kindly let me pass. The snaky, dragony creature just lay

there blocking my path, flaming from one end, smoking from the other.

I was groaning with hunger, aching with it. The Good Fairy's house could not be far away now, so I decided that instead of waiting around for the dragony snake to move, I'd leave the muddy road and find my way back home across country. So that's what I did.

I hadn't gone many miles before I came upon a vineyard. A vineyard! Grapes! Big, red, luscious grapes everywhere, all around me. No one was around. No one would miss a few grapes, surely. So I helped myself, stuffed myself full of grapes. Nothing had ever tasted better, not even cake.

What a stroke of luck, I thought, to have met that snaky, dragony thing, and to have had to turn off the road into the fields. Things were looking up at last, really looking up.

"Thank you, thank you!" I cried out loud in my joy.

To my surprise a crowd of crows cawed back at me. "Look out! Look out!" they cawed.

Too late!

I heard a crack, like a pistol shot, like a branch breaking —no, it was more like a leg breaking. I looked down.

My leg!

I had stepped right into a trap and could not move. My poor wooden leg was broken. I felt the pain burning up my body, as if I was on fire.

I screamed, I yelled, but no help came. I tried to pry open the trap, but I couldn't budge it. I was stuck fast. I would die here all alone. My head began to swim. "Mama, Papa, sweet sister," I could only whisper, I was so weak. "Help me, help me, please."

No one came because no one heard me. I was alone in the darkness and had just about given up all hope, when I saw a flickering light in the dark.

A flitting firefly!

I reached out and touched her as she flew near.

"Oh, please set me free," I begged her.

The Flitting Firefly flew all around me, shining her light on me, on my leg, on the trap.

"What happened?" she asked me.

"I was just eating a few grapes," I told her.

"Stealing a few grapes, you mean, you naughty little puppet," the Flitting Firefly said.

"But I was hungry," I protested. "Why does everyone I meet try to tell me what I should and shouldn't do? You sound just like the Talking Cricket. Please might we discuss the rights and wrongs of this later? My leg is hurting me like crazy! Please just get me out of here."

"That's no excuse for taking what is not yours—you should know that. You must live and learn from your mistakes," said the Flitting Firefly.

That was when I heard footsteps coming toward us through the darkness.

"This is the farmer whose grapes you were stealing, you naughty little puppet," said the firefly. "You'd better ask him to help you, though I see no reason why he should. Here he comes."

And sure enough I saw the light of a lantern dancing toward us through the darkness, and heavy feet stomping along with it.

"Caught you, you rascally weasel," came a gruff voice. The light of the lantern fell on me. He bent down closer to get a better look at me.

"Oh, so you're not a weasel after all, are you?

You're a boy, a puppety sort of boy, if I'm not mistaken, but a boy all the same. And there was I thinking it was weasels that were stealing my chickens. It was you all along!"

"I never," I cried. "I just ate four grapes."

"Grape thief? Chicken thief?" he roared. "What's the difference? Either way you need to be taught a lesson. Weasels are thieves; it's in their nature. Boys like you should know better."

And with that he grabbed me by the neck, opened the trap, and lifted me out. I wiggled and kicked, but it was no good. He had a grip of steel around my throat, almost throttling me.

"I shall set you to work right away," he said. "Due punishment for stealing my grapes. Only last week my poor old guard dog, Melempo, died—the best, most trusted friend I ever had—and I haven't got around to getting another one to take his place. So, you'll have to do. From now on, you'll be my guard dog. You'll sleep in Melempo's doghouse out near the chicken coop, and if any weasels come along you'll bark like crazy and I'll come running with my gun. Understood?"

So that's how I found myself that night, chained up in Melempo's doghouse, guarding the farmer's chickens. Try as I did, I could not break free of my collar and chain. I lay there on the straw, the Flitting Firefly's words echoing in my head. *You must live and learn from your mistakes. You must live and learn.*

"I will, little firefly," I said out loud, hoping she was still somewhere near and would hear me. "I will, really truly."

Filled with shame and regret and sadness—and feeling

very sorry for myself altogether, I cried myself to sleep.

I was woken up in the middle of the night by the sound of hushed whisperings. One look out of my kennel told me what was there.

Weasels, four of them, by the chicken run.

They were trying to dig themselves in under the wire.

And I was supposed to be the guard dog.

"You!" I cried. "What are you up to? Go away or I shall bark and wake my master up."

The four weasels trotted over to me and looked me up and down.

"Goodness, Melempo," said one, "you're a lot thinner all of a sudden."

"I'm not Melempo," I said. "Melempo died last week, and I'm just taking his place for the night."

"He's a very skinny-looking dog," said another weasel.

"And he looks a bit wooden to me," said another, peering closely at me.

"I am not a dog. I am Pinocchio. I am a puppet. I'm just playing at being a guard dog for the night. The farmer said I had to bark if any weasely thieves came to steal away his hens. And it looks to me as if you might be the thieves he was talking about."

The weasels looked at one another, and then tapping their noses conspiratorially, they whispered: "Psst! Listen, Pinocchio, can we do a deal here? With Melempo, we had this arrangement…."

"What arrangement?"

"Well, he turned a blind eye, kept shtoom, while we dug under the wire and helped ourselves to a chicken each, and we always made sure we gave Melempo one too, a nice fat one for his breakfast. That was the deal. So everyone was happy. What do you say? Can we rely on you, Pinocchio?"

I did not like the look of these thieving weasels, not one bit. They had wicked, weasely eyes and twisty smiles. An idea came into my head, a canny idea, I thought.

"I'll tell you what," I said, "I'll do better than Melempo."

I stood up in the mouth of my kennel. "If my chain reaches that far, and I think it will, I will open the gate of the chicken run and let you in. Then you won't have to dig your way under the wire, will you?"

"No barking?" they asked me.

"Of course not," I replied, walking toward the gate. My chain, I discovered was just long enough to open the gate for them.

"In you go," I said, letting them in. "And good hunting!"

I could hear the hens fluttering and squawking in the chicken coop as they heard the wicked weasels stealing across the run toward them. Then I slammed the gate shut behind them and locked it fast. Then I barked, well, sort of. Actually, I shouted, I yelled, "Mr. Farmer, I've caught the weasels for you, locked them up in the chicken run. Come quickly!"

Out came the farmer, running across the farmyard in his nightshirt, a blunderbuss in his hand.

The weasels tried to escape, but there was nowhere to run to. *Bang! Bang! Bang! Bang!* Dead as doornails, every one of them.

"You brave boy," said the farmer, patting me on the head just as if I was a real dog. "You saved my hens. You saved my eggs. You are a better guard dog than Melempo ever was."

Better than you know, Mr. Farmer, I thought.

I did think of telling him how Melempo had been in league with the wicked weasels all these years. But then I thought, *What's the point?* He'd loved his old dog, his best friend in all the world, he'd said. So I only told the farmer half the story, how the weasels had tried to bribe me not to bark.

"I may be a bit of a rascal, sir," I said. "I pinched a few grapes, maybe, but I'm not that much of a rascal."

"Indeed not," said the farmer, slipping the collar off my neck. "You are a fine boy. Anyone would be proud to have you for a son or a brother or a friend. You have a nice snooze now in my nice warm farmhouse, and then, once it's light, I'll give you a good hearty breakfast and send you on your way."

CHAPTER EIGHT

All alone in the world

So, in the morning, I was on my way again. I had had enough of adventures by now. I just wanted to find my Good Fairy's cottage again, to be with her, and with Mama and Papa.

I walked and walked. After a while I began to recognize where I was. I came across the tree where I'd so nearly been hanged. But however hard I searched I couldn't find the little white cottage where the Good Fairy had taken me in and looked after me.

By the time darkness fell I was completely exhausted and could walk no farther. I curled up under a tree. An owl hooted above me, little creatures rustled and rooted around in the forest. But nothing could keep me awake.

How I wish I had never fallen asleep! For I dreamed the worst dream I had ever had. I was searching through the forest and came at last to the ruins of the Good Fairy's cottage—and nearby a marble stone.

I went closer.

It was a gravestone. The words I read on it broke my heart.

"Here lies the Good Fairy with the sea-blue hair.
She died from grief after her beloved little
brother Pinocchio ran away and abandoned her."

I woke myself up sobbing. "Please don't let it be true," I cried. "I did abandon her, and I abandoned Papa and Mama too. Maybe they're dead as well. Oh, please don't let it be true."

Just then a cooing pigeon fluttered down and landed beside me.

"What's up?" he cooed. "You seem awfully upset."

So, as you sometimes do with strangers, I told him my whole story, and all about the terrible dream I'd just had.

"So you are the famous Pinocchio," he said, nodding away as pigeons do. "I've heard of you. Everyone is looking for you, you know. Your Mama has stayed at home waiting for you, in case you return. And Gepetto, your Papa, travels the country far and wide asking around for you, searching for you.

He even asks pigeons like me if we've seen you. Yes, you are the most famous puppet in the world."

"You know Papa?" I cried.

"Of course," the Cooing Pigeon said. "Actually, I last saw him down by the sea, only three or four days ago. He was building a boat on a beach. As soon as it's finished he's going to sail off across the seas to look for you. He told me he thought you might have been captured by pirates."

"Is this beach far away?" I asked him.

"Nowhere's that far when you can fly," the Cooing Pigeon replied. "I could fly you there if you like. Maybe he's still making his boat. Maybe he hasn't sailed yet."

"You could fly me there?" I said. "That would be wonderful. But won't I be too heavy?"

"You, heavy?" he cooed. "There's practically

nothing of you. Hop on, Pinocchio. And hang on tight. We'll be there before you know it, lickety-split."

So I hopped on and hung on, and off and away we flew, up over the forests and fields, following a winding river down toward the sea.

It was cold high up there, in and out of the clouds, so I buried myself in the Cooing Pigeon's feathers to try to keep warm, closed my eyes against the rushing of the wind, praying and praying that we wouldn't be too late, that Papa had not yet set sail.

"Look down there!" cooed the pigeon.

From far away we could see the beach and the cliffs, crowded with tiny people. But there was no sign of a boat, not on the beach or out at sea. All we could see were the heaving waves and the stormy horizon.

By this time the poor Cooing Pigeon was quite exhausted. He only just managed to make it as far as the beach. As we landed, we saw that everyone was pointing seawards.

"He's out there, that brave old man, setting sail in

a storm like this to find his long lost son. How brave is that?"

Catching a glimpse of a white sail in the waves, I ran to the water's edge waving and shouting, "I'm here, Papa! I'm here!" But the wind blew my words away.

Again and again we glimpsed the sail, and every time a great shout went up, "Come back, old man! He's here! Pinocchio is here on the beach."

And then a great towering wave reared up and I saw Papa's little boat rising, rising, then crashing down, turning upside down. Now there was no sail to see any more, and the wailing of everyone on the beach filled the air. The gulls cried, and the wind whined.

All I knew was that Papa was somewhere in that heaving sea and that I must save him. I rushed down to the water's edge and I dove headlong into the waves.

As I swam, I looked for Papa from the top of every wave. But I never saw his sail again, nor any other sign of him.

Night came on and all there was around me was the darkness of the sea.

It rained and it hailed. Thunder rumbled. Lightning crackled.

I cried out for the Good Fairy, but no help came. I was tossed around the ocean like a bobbing cork and had no strength to swim any more. All I could do was to keep floating until daylight came. I had to keep hoping, hoping for a boat to rescue me, or to be washed up on a shore somewhere.

By first light I found myself being tumbled around in raging, roaring surf. Ahead of me I could see rearing rocks. I would be smashed to pieces!

A great
wave took
me and hurled
me up high. I
shut my eyes and
prepared for the
worst. But when I
landed, I found myself
on a beach of soft sand.
I sat there, stunned and
bewildered. I had survived!
I was alive!

It was as if the page had suddenly turned. The sun came through the storm clouds, the sea calmed. I shivered the cold out of me, laid out my wet clothes to dry and thanked my lucky stars—and my dear, Good Fairy—for saving me.

I was on an island, a paradise of white sand and waving palm trees, with parrots all the colors of the rainbow flitting through the branches. Out at sea there were soaring gulls and diving gannets, but no sails.

Papa was not out there.

No one was out there.

I had been saved, but I was all alone.

I was hungry too again. To be lonely and hungry, there is nothing worse. My relief and happiness at being alive soon gave way to tears of despair. I sat on the beach and cried my heart out.

"Why so downhearted?" came a voice from the sea.

I looked up. It was a smiling dolphin, close to the shore and talking to me.

"I'm all alone," I said.

"You're not," he replied—he had gentle, kind eyes. "I'm here. How can I help you?"

"Well," I told him, "I am ever so hungry. Where can I find something to eat?"

"Go along the beach toward the rising sun," said the Smiling Dolphin. "It's a bit of a way, but as you go, follow your nose. You'll find the air will be sweeter with every step, as sweet as honey."

My mouth watered at the thought of it.

"'Scuse me," I said. "In your travels around the ocean, you haven't by any chance seen my Papa, have you? He was out in the storm last night looking for me.

In a little boat with a white sail."

The Smiling Dolphin shook his head and tutted as dolphins do. "Not a good night to be out, not in a storm like that, and not with the Giant Gruesome Shark around."

"Giant Gruesome Shark?" I cried.

"You wouldn't want to meet him on a dark night, I can tell you," said the Smiling Dolphin. "He is mean as well as huge and gruesome. He's been known to swallow warships and whaling boats—whole! Just opens his giant mouth and gobbles them up. Not nice! I don't want to worry you, though."

And off the Smiling Dolphin swam out to sea, leaving me standing there, not just worried but terrified for my poor Papa.

If he had been gobbled up it would have been all my fault. He'd been out there in the boat looking for me. He might still be. Yes, he might still be! *Don't be downhearted*, I told myself. *Find some food—that'll make you feel better.*

So I followed my nose along the beach as the Smiling Dolphin had told me, and, just as he had said, the air was sweet with the scent of honey.

At last I came to a village. There were people out in the streets hurrying and scurrying hither and thither. A coal merchant passed me, carrying a heavy sack of coal. "What is this place?" I asked, catching up to him.

"The Village of Busy Bees," he replied.

"I'm so hungry," I said. "And I smell honey. Where can I get some?"

"You'll need money to buy it," he said gruffly. "Here, carry my sack for a while and I'll give you a penny or two for your work...."

"Not likely," I told him. "What do you think I am, a donkey?"

"Please yourself," he said. "No money, no honey. Simple as that."

I wandered on through the bustling streets and came across a bricklayer humping a sack of plaster. "Here, lad," he said. "Give us a hand, will you? I'll pay you decent money. I'm getting a bit old these days for this hard work."

"Do I look like a carthorse?" I said. "Why does everyone in this village want to treat me like a pack animal? I can't carry that. It's far too heavy and I'm too little. All I want is a big, big spoonful of that honey I can smell."

"Suit yourself," the bricklayer said. "No money, no honey. That's life. Very simple."

A little farther on, I met a bent old woman in a black bonnet carrying two water jugs. That reminded me—I wasn't just hungry, I was thirsty too.

"Can I have a drink, please," I asked her.

"Of course, dear," said the old lady. "Help yourself."

It was delicious water and I drank it until both jugs were empty. But I was still dying of hunger.

"You haven't by any chance got any honey, have you?" I asked her.

"No, dear," she replied. "But I've got some bread at home if you'd like that?"

I thought that I recognized her voice, but I couldn't remember ever having seen her before.

"If you wouldn't mind carrying these two big jugs home for me, then I'd be pleased to let you have some of my bread."

"No honey?"

"No honey. But I can make you some nice cauliflower and cheese, and afterwards maybe some bread and jam."

She made it sound so delicious I would have carried a dozen elephants home for her! So I carried her jugs home, one on top of the other on my head. She lived in a little house on the edge of the village.

As soon as we got there, she sat me down at her table and gave me the best, most welcome supper I've ever had: cauliflower and cheese and bread and jam. I devoured everything she put before me, licked the plate clean! Not a crumb was left.

"Thank you, thank you," I said, and as I spoke, the bent old lady took off her bonnet. Her hair was sea blue! And her wrinkled skin became smooth as she stood straight and tall. She was the Good Fairy, my beloved sister, not dead as I had thought, but alive, alive!

I leapt up from the table and hugged her to me.

So that's how I came to find my dear sister, the Good Fairy, in the Village of Busy Bees.

She took me in, fed me, clothed me, and comforted me when I was sad. And I was often sad, especially at night when I couldn't sleep. I missed Papa and Mama dreadfully. Papa I knew by now I would never see again. But I determined I would go home and be with Mama again, and I would take the Good Fairy, my dear sister, with me, and we would be a family together.

"One day all will be well again, Pinocchio, I promise you," she said. "But meanwhile you will have to go to school like other boys do, and work hard as everyone does in this village, children and grown-up children alike."

"But, dear sister, I hate work," I told her. "It's hard. It's difficult."

"I know," she told me, "but work can also be fun, you'll see."

The Good Fairy was right about most things, I knew

that, but not about this. What she didn't understand was that I liked lolling around; playing with the toys she gave me; enjoying myself.

"Pinocchio," she said, "you have a kind heart, and I love you, but you are sometimes a bit lazy. So I want you to go to school, work hard, do your best and make me proud of you."

It took her a while to persuade me—the idea of school did not appeal to me one bit. But I did want to make her proud of me.

"I promise I will work hard, dear sister," I told her. "I won't let you down this time, I promise."

That's the trouble with promises. I always found them so easy to make, and so hard to keep.

So she sent me off to school in the Village of Busy Bees, where the children, I soon discovered, worked just as hard as everyone else in the village; and these goody-goodies expected me to do the same. But worst of all, just like the boys in my old school, they teased me all the time. They called me "wooden top" or "blockhead."

I had only one friend in the whole school. He was called Lampwick because he was so skinny and tall. He never teased me, not once. He was just about as naughty as me too, so for once I had a partner in crime.

Our horrible teacher, Mr. Beaky, was always standing Lampwick in the corner. When my writing or my math wasn't good enough, Mr. Beaky would tick me off and stand me in the corner too.

Actually I didn't mind that much, because Lampwick was usually there. I liked being in the corner with

Lampwick. We'd wink at each other and turn around and put our tongues out at the other children when Mr. Beaky wasn't looking.

Day after day the others went on teasing me, just because I nodded my head or jiggled around when I moved. In the playground sometimes they'd play at being puppets and join hands circling me, clumping their feet as I did and laughing at me. It made me so angry.

I told my Good Fairy about it and she said they'd soon get tired of it, that I mustn't take any notice, and certainly not get into any fights about it. "You just have to work hard, Pinocchio, and show them you're no blockhead, that you're as good as they are, better even."

I liked that idea. Yes, I would show them. I'd be

better than them at everything. I would settle down, go to school every day, be on time, and work so hard that I'd amaze both the teachers and the other children. And that's just what I did.

Soon I was top of the class, top goody-goody in the whole school. But it wasn't long before I discovered, of course, that that didn't make me many friends, either. Quite the opposite—they picked on me more than ever.

I'd had enough of all their mocking antics. When one big bully boy shouted at me, "You're nothing but a walking skeleton, Pinocchio. Rattlebones! Rattlebones!" I did what the Good Fairy said and tried to take no notice. But when he said it again and tweaked my nose, I went for him. I didn't care how big and strong he was.

I kicked him with my hard little feet.

I punched him with my hard little fists and I butted him with my hard little head.

Everyone gathered around, and a great shout went up.

"Fight! Fight! Come on, Pinocchio!" They were cheering for me!

When I'd finished all my punching and kicking I sat on the big bully boy and raised my fists in the air.

"Champion!" they cried. "Pinocchio's a champion!"

After that I was the flavor of the month. Everyone wanted to be my best friend. They all wanted to play the games I wanted to play. I was the most popular boy in the whole school. I was King of the Castle, top dog, and I was loving every minute of it. I didn't have to work hard any more to prove myself. It was all too easy to give up being the hard-working schoolboy I had become. Being popular was far more fun, and I could see that what made me really popular was fighting.

By now I was in with a crowd of bad boys. I was their gang leader. We skipped off school whenever we could. So that's how we ended up down on the beach that morning, me and my gang, instead of being at school.

We didn't start the fight, but we finished it.

A gang of boys ambushed us in the dunes. They snatched our school books and we went after them. I was a fearless fighter by now, and the fastest runner. So I caught up with them first.

It was quite a punch-up, fists and feet flying everywhere. But I had wooden feet, wooden fists, and they hurt!

It wasn't long before we had them on the run. As we chased after them along the beach I picked up the heaviest book I could find—they were scattered all over the sand—and hurled it after them.

It hit one of the boys on the back of the head and knocked him senseless to the ground.

He was out cold.

"Run and get some water," I said. Lampwick rushed off and filled his hat from the sea.

We splashed water on the boy's face to wake him up.

We shook him.

But nothing did any good.

"You've killed him, Pinocchio!" Lampwick cried, and then he and all my friends—if you can call them that—ran away.

So there I was, left alone on the beach with this boy, suddenly realizing what I had done, regretting everything I'd become, and knowing how much I had let myself down again, how much of a disappointment I must be to my Good Fairy, just as I had been to my dear Mama and Papa.

I was trying to shake some life into the boy, when along came two *Carabinieri*—two of the most fearsome policemen I'd ever seen—with a monster of a dog that bared his teeth at me and growled most horribly.

"What happened here, young fellow-me-lad?" one of them asked me. "Did you do this?"

"No, I never," I told them. "This book," I picked up one of the books and showed it to them, "it just…well, it just hit him."

"Whose book is it, young fellow-me-lad?"

"Mine."

Just then the boy sat up and rubbed his head.

"Where am I?" he said.

Then he recognized me and saw the *Carabinieri.* "He done it," the boy shouted, pointing at me, "he hit me. I could've been killed. Arrest him! Arrest him! Put him in prison!"

Well I'd already been in prison—you know that— and I didn't want to go there ever again. So I ran.

No puppet ever ran faster than I did then, and that was because, every time I looked around, that great slobbery monster of a dog was hard on my heels, and his teeth looked very big and very sharp.

But no matter how fast I ran, he was running faster. He was catching up on me all the time. I could feel his hot breath on my neck. Any moment now I'd feel his teeth sinking into me. He'd tear me to pieces and spit me out on the sand, and that would be the end of Pinocchio.

CHAPTER NINE

Out of the jaws of death and into another frying pan

I had no choice. I was fast running out of beach.

Ahead of me the cliff face rose sheer out of the sand, impossible to climb. The slavering beast was so close now I could feel his slobber dribbling down the back of my neck.

I jinked this way and that, and then, changing direction suddenly, made a dash for the sea. I plunged into the waves and swam out as fast and as far as I could. Behind me I heard a great kerfuffle of splashing and baying and whining as if a hundred dogs were after me.

When I looked back over my shoulder, I could see the dog was in trouble. He was floundering, his paws flailing in the water. He kept sinking below the waves and bobbing up again, gasping for air.

"I'm drowning," he cried. "Help me, please."

To be honest, at first I was rather pleased he was drowning. I mean, after all, only a few moments before he'd been doing his best to catch me and tear me into little pieces. But then I heard the Good Fairy's voice in my head.

Be kind, brother dear, be kind. You can't leave him to drown.

She was right of course, she was always right.

"All right," I said, swimming back toward the dog. "But

if I rescue you, you won't come after me again, will you?"

"I promise," the poor dog spluttered. "Quickly, Pinocchio, or I'll drown before you get to me."

It was safest to grab him by the tail—it was the other end from his jaws after all. Towing him behind me, I swam with the current, around the headland, and came close enough to the rocky shore for him to be able to find his feet and clamber out. But I kept a safe distance, treading water. He looked very big again, now he was out of danger, and I didn't quite trust him. He stood there looking down at me, shaking himself dry.

"I am Alidoro," he said. "You have been a good friend to me, Pinocchio, and I shall not forget it."

But I decided to stay in the water as long as I possibly could until I was sure that both he and those two *Carabinieri* had gone.

It must have been at least half an hour and there was no further sign of them. The coast was clear and I began to swim ashore.

I had almost reached dry land when I felt myself suddenly caught up in a net and being hauled toward the shore. And I wasn't alone—there were hundreds of fish of all sizes and colors all around me: mackerel, red mullet, salmon, anchovies, cod, crabs, lobsters; all of us crushed together and struggling to break free.

Up, out of the sea we were hauled, helpless and breathless in the net, to find the great ugly face of a fisherman looking down at us and grinning from ear to ear when he saw what a catch he had. And when I say ugly, I mean ugly. He was green from head to toe—skin, hair, eyes, all green, like a giant lizard.

"Aha!" he hissed—he spoke like a lizard too. "Aha!

What fine fish I have caught, what a meal I will be having today."

He threw us together inside a basket and carried us off to his cottage.

Here he pulled us out one by one. "I'll fry this mullet," he said, "boil this lobster and I'll smoke this salmon. What a feast of fish I shall have."

And then he had me by the leg and was dangling me in the air.

"What is this?" he said. I could see when he spoke he had a green tongue too—I'd never seen anyone with a green tongue before. "A strange woodeny-looking sort of crabby fish. I'll put him in with the lobster to boil."

"No, no," I cried. "Don't boil me! You can't eat me! I'm a puppet."

"A puppet fish!" he replied. "I've never heard of such a thing. But since you can talk as I do, and that is quite unusual for a fish, I shall treat you with respect. You may choose how you wish to be cooked: fried in a pan with butter, perhaps, or cooked slowly in onion, garlic and tomato sauce?"

"To be honest, sir," I told him, being polite only because I was scared rigid, "I'd really rather not be cooked at all. I'd very much rather be set free so I can go home."

"Oh, I'm afraid I can't let you do that," he said. "I've never seen a puppet fish before, let alone a talking one. You're a very rare species you know, and I'd like to know what you taste like. I'll put you in the frying pan with the mullet and the mackerel, with a little butter and parsley. You'll like it, you'll enjoy it; you'll

be frying in good company after all."

Did I squeal then, and struggle and squirm? I should say I did. Did my whole life flash before me as he tied me hand and foot? All the silly, selfish things I'd done were played out in my mind, in my stupid wooden head. I'd never see my Good Fairy again, my Mama, my Papa. If only, if only...

Then he was dipping me in a batter of egg and flour, laying me out in a great platter alongside the mullet and the mackerel. I smelled the butter melting in the pan, heard it bubbling, saw the smoke rising.

The mackerel went in first and sizzled, then the mullet, and sizzled. Now I was the only one left on the platter.

Now it was my turn to be sizzled.

The green-eyed fisherman laughed in my face as he bent over me. "What a funny-looking little fish you are. You're so ugly you make me laugh. You make me laugh! I hope you taste better than you look."

Then he reached out and grabbed me by the head.

So this is how you end up, Pinocchio, I told myself. *As fish and chips, Pinocchio and chips. What a way to go.*

At that very moment, the moment of my almost being Pinocchio Frittata—well I am an Italian puppet, you know—a huge dog came bounding into the fisherman's cottage. You've guessed it, it was Alidoro!

"I'll have that fish of yours, you green-eyed ogre," he barked. "Puppet fish is my favorite."

The fisherman kicked out at him. "Out of here, you mutt," he roared.

At this Alidoro lifted his lips and snarled at him. "Drop that puppet fish," he said between bared teeth, "before I lose my temper and chomp you into little green pieces."

That was enough for the fisherman. He let go at once and I fell into Alidoro's open jaws, landing on his soft warm tongue. And off he ran with me in his mouth.

That dog was so kind. First he licked all the batter off me, then he dunked me again and again in the sea until I was completely rinsed and then made me gallop alongside him up and down the beach to dry me off.

"There," he said. "You look more like your old self again."

"Thank you, dear Alidoro," I said as I shook him politely by his huge paw, "Thank you!"

"What else are friends for?" he replied. "Didn't you

save me? Off you go, little puppet friend, go straight home and try to keep out of trouble from now on, all right? There's a good puppet."

And off he trotted, wagging his goodbyes as he went.

It was night-time before I saw the flickering lights of the Good Fairy's house. Was I glad to be home! In that one day I'd had quite enough adventures for a lifetime.

But when I stood at her front door, longing only to be inside and see her again, I found I couldn't bring myself to knock. I couldn't face her, not after what I'd done. What would I say? "I'm sorry, sister, after all you've done for me, I let you down again, I broke my promises again." If she turned me away I wouldn't have blamed her.

So instead of waking her up, I lay down on the front-door step and spent all night thinking about how silly I'd been, how lucky I was to have survived and how I must learn from my mistakes this time.

So that's where the Good Fairy found me the next morning, fast asleep on her doorstep, and that's how come the first thing I said to her was—in the midst of my tears—"Please forgive me, sister dear. I shan't go running off again. I shall study hard, go to school every day. This I promise you faithfully."

There were no angry words from her, no lectures. She forgave me at once, hugged me to her, took me inside and fed me a huge breakfast of pancakes and honey.

Then, just as she sent me off to school, she said, "Pinocchio, I have an idea. Tomorrow we shall have a party for all your school friends to celebrate your return and new beginning. Would you like that?"

"A party, dear sister," I cried. "How wonderful! Lampwick will come, everyone will come. I have forgiven them now for running off as they did. I'd have probably done the same thing. I can't wait to see them again."

They were all there, all my friends, at the school gates and they greeted me like a conquering hero, all except the teachers of course. And the more I told Lampwick and my friends of my adventures with the *Carabinieri*, Alidoro and the green fisherman, the more popular I became.

"And you're all invited to my party," I told them. "My Good Fairy has promised it will be the best party ever—costumes, cake, cotton candy, ice cream, and all

the games you can think of too: catch, hide-and-seek,

blind man's buff. You name it, we'll play it."

"We'll come, we'll come," they all shouted, leaping

up and down in delight. "When is it?"

"Tomorrow," I told them. But as we walked home after school that day I could tell that Lampwick was a bit down in the dumps.

"Don't you want to come to my party?" I asked him.

"I won't be here," he said. "I'm off. I've had enough of school and teachers. One party isn't enough, Pinocchio, I want every day to be a party. No more books, no more work. Just fun, that's all I want."

He leaned over and whispered to me, "I'm not supposed to tell anyone. This man said I had to keep it a secret, but you're my best friend, Pinocchio, so I'll tell you. I don't want to leave you behind. I want you to come with me!"

"Where?" I asked him. "What are you talking about?"

"This man, he's coming with his wagon tonight, and I'm going."

"Going where?"

"To the Land of Toys, Pinocchio," he replied, "where every day is a holiday, from the first of January to the last day in December. Every day is Saturday and Sunday, can you imagine that? All day, every day, we just play and party. You stay here and you'll just have one party and then it'll be back to boring old school again. Come with me to the Land of Toys, Pinocchio."

"I can't," I told him. "I promised the Good Fairy, my dear kind sister, who's been so good to me, that I will go to school, and do my work, and I'll never run away again."

"Boring, boring Pinocchio. Life is for living, for fun, not for working."

I couldn't stop thinking about this Land of Toys. "Are there really no teachers there?" I asked Lampwick.

"Not one."

"And every day really is a holiday? Truly?"

"Every day."

"Are you quite sure, Lampwick?"

"Cross my heart and hope to die."

"When are you going?"

"As soon as the wagon comes along. Won't be long, now. Come on, Pinocchio, we're best friends, aren't we? Best friends stick together, don't they? It'll be an adventure, Pinocchio, and you like adventures, don't you?"

"What about my party?" I said. "I'll miss my party. What about the Good Fairy—she'll be so upset."

At that moment we heard a bell tinkling in the distance, and saw the glow of a lantern far off down the road.

"It's the wagon," said Lampwick. "Make up your
mind, Pinocchio. It's now or never. A life of fun in
the Land of Toys, or one lousy party with blind man's
bluff and a miserable bit of cake, and teachers and

dunces' hats and standing in the corner. Take your pick, Pinocchio."

So I took my pick, didn't I? Even as I was waiting for the wagon to come along and pick us up I knew I was doing the wrong thing, but I did it all the same. And as usual I lived to regret it. I was soon to find out what a stupid donkey I had been, and just what a stupid donkey I was to become.

CHAPTER TEN

The Land of Toys

It was the strangest wagon; it made no noise on the road, as if it were a ghost wagon, and it was pulled by five pairs of donkeys: two gray, six piebald, and a pair that had stripes and looked more like zebras.

Weirdest of all, though, was the driver, a little fat man in a pixie cap. From the first moment I saw him I didn't trust him. When he smiled he didn't mean it. When he talked, he mewed like a cat—

I didn't like that, either!

Behind him I could see the wagon was full of children, all of them jostling and singing, happy as larks.

"We're off to the Land of Toys," mewed the Little Fat Man. "Hop on, sweet children! Hop on! Come with us and be happy forever."

"You see?" said Lampwick. "It's true, Pinocchio. Everything I told you is true."

But I couldn't make up my mind.

"I'm not sure," I told him, turning away. "What would my Good Fairy say? It'll break her heart if I run away again."

"Well, are you coming, or aren't you? We haven't got all day," mewed the Little Fat Man irritably. I noticed then that he had sharp little eyes like a ferret, a hunter's eyes. "You can ride up on that stripy donkey if you like. Ice cream when we get there: strawberry, chocolate, all you can eat."

In one jump Lampwick was up astride one of the donkeys.

"Come on, Pinocchio," Lampwick cried, holding out his hand to me. "What are we waiting for? Do you hear that? All the ice cream you can eat."

The other children in the cart were egging me on. "Jump up, Pinocchio, don't miss the fun, come with us."

I thought once—*no*—twice—*no*—three times—*yes, yes, yes*. And up I jumped on to the donkey, to a great cheer from the wagon. I sat there next to Lampwick as we rode off, away from my home and the Good Fairy, off to the Land of Toys.

Sad to say, very soon I had forgotten all about my promise, and found myself singing along with the others: "If you're happy and you know it clap your hands."

And as we clapped our hands, the donkeys picked up their feet and trotted on into the night. Looking around behind me I noticed that the driver, the Little Fat Man with the pixie cap, was smiling from ear to ear, as happy as a mouse in cheese, as a cat in cream.

Then I heard a voice. At first I thought it was the Good Fairy whispering to me as she sometimes did inside my head, but it wasn't her.

It was the donkey I was riding, the stripy donkey.

"Don't do it," he whispered. "Jump off now, go home before it is too late, before—"

"Shut up, donkey!" screeched the driver and he lashed out with his whip. "No talking, just pull, you stupid beast, pull!" And the donkey never spoke again.

He cried, though, I know he did. I saw the tears.

"Did you hear that, Lampwick?" I asked. "Did you hear what the donkey said?"

"Donkeys are like that," said Lampwick. "They always look on the dark side of life, always gloomy. Take no notice."

"Take no notice," echoed the Little Fat Man from

behind me. "We'll be in the Land of Toys by morning, and the land of ice cream, too, don't forget that." And he whipped my donkey on again.

"The donkey is crying," I protested. "You shouldn't whip him like that."

"And why not?" replied the driver. "A donkey is a donkey is a donkey. I don't care about donkeys. I care about children like you, my dear. I want to give you a happy time, the happiest time you ever had. You know what our motto is in the Land of Toys: *Have Fun, Be Happy!* You'll see what I mean, my dear, as soon as we get there."

I was sorry for the donkey, sorry too to be leaving home, but I couldn't help wondering about this Land of Toys. If it was true, everything I'd heard about it, then what a life I'd have—all I wanted, all I'd ever dreamed of.

From the moment I first set eyes on the Land of Toys, I knew Lampwick had been right. The Little Fat Man who drove the wagon—even if I didn't like the look of him—had been as good as his word.

The streets were filled with laughing children, dancing, singing, playing all manner of games: marbles, jacks, skipping. There were children in costumes everywhere—pirates and princesses, soldiers and sailors, knights and dragons. There were posters up all over the town: *"No school here"*, *"No need to work"*, *"Have Fun, Be Happy!"*

I saw only two kinds of shop—toy shops and candy shops—and every candy shop had an ice-cream stand outside.

"All candy is free, all ice cream is free," laughed the Little Fat Man. "Off you get. Enjoy yourselves, my

dears. Have fun, be happy." And when he laughed, he cackled like a crow. *Caw! Caw! Caw!*

But I paid little attention to that.

Like all the children, Lampwick and I were soon caught up in the fun. We did as we pleased, ran wild on the streets, stuffed ourselves with candy and ice cream, as much as we wanted. We stayed up as late as we liked, had bonfire parties every night, with sausages and tomato sauce, and marshmallows roasted in the fire.

Day after day Lampwick asked me the same question: "Well, Pinocchio, dear friend, was I right or was I wrong? Aren't you glad you came away with me? Be honest now, do you ever think of home or that Good Fairy of yours?"

And the awful truth was—and believe me, I'm not

proud of it—that I never did. I was far too busy having fun, being happy.

"Do you remember that silly old goat Mr. Beaky, at school, who was always punishing us?" I said. "He used to tell me I should keep away from you, that friends like you were no good for me."

"Funny," laughed Lampwick. "He said exactly the same thing to me about you. Silly old goat!"

Weeks, months went by, and so fast because we were having the time of our lives. But truth be told, I was getting just a little fed up with ice cream and candy and sausages; and occasionally at night I did begin to wonder how my Good Fairy was, and Mama and Papa. But come the next morning, I'd very soon forget all about them again.

Then one morning I woke up feeling rather odd. I remembered I'd been dreaming I was a stripy donkey with long ears. I suppose that was why, when I woke up, I found myself fingering my ears.

At first I thought I must be still inside my dream.

But I wasn't! This was real!

My ears weren't like mine at all, not small and wooden, but long and hairy!

I sprang out of bed and ran to look at myself in the mirror. I could hardly believe my eyes. I knocked my hand against the wall to be sure I was really awake.

I was! I was!

Even as I looked at myself in the mirror, my ears kept growing longer, hairier, *donkier*.

I shrieked so loudly that my next-door neighbor, a dozy dormouse, came running in. "What's up, Pinocchio?" he cried.

And then he saw my ears.

"Oh no," said the Dozy Dormouse.

He felt my forehead.

"Oh no," he said again. "I'm afraid you have the dreaded fever."

"What fever?" I asked.

"Donkey fever. I'm sorry to have to tell you that sooner or later all the children catch it. In just a few hours you will become a donkey. There's no cure, nothing anyone can do. It starts with the ears—the rest soon follows. You'll be a donkey, just like the ones who brought you here in the wagon. They were all children once."

I cried bitter tears. "It's not true," I wailed, grasping my ears and trying to pull them off. "Please tell me it's not true!"

"I've seen it all before. All you children are the same—boys more than girls, I have to say—you think you can have what you like in life without working for it."

The Dozy Dormouse wagged his little paw at me. "You should have stayed at school and studied, you should have stayed at home. I can't help you now. No one can."

"It's all my friend's fault; it's Lampwick's fault," I told him.

"No, it's not. It's your own fault, Pinocchio. What you do is up to you and no one else." And he scuttled away, leaving me alone with my donkey ears.

Lampwick got me into this, I thought. *Lampwick can get me out of it.*

But I couldn't show myself in the streets looking like this. Everyone would laugh at me. So I found a brown paper bag to disguise myself. And then I ran, tripping and stumbling as I went, across the road and into his house.

I didn't knock, I just burst in.

Lampwick was sitting in his chair by the fire, a paper bag just like mine over his head. We looked at one another.

"Is everything all right?" I said.

"Fine," he replied. "Just perfect. Why?"

"Then how come you've got a paper bag on your head?" I asked.

"I could ask you the same question," he replied.

"Earache," I told him. "Doctor's orders. He said a paper bag would make it better."

"That's funny," he replied. "I've got earache too. Which is your bad ear?"

"Both," I said.

"Me too," he mumbled, and then nervously,

"Pinocchio, can I see your ears, please?"

"I want to see yours first."

"No, yours."

"Yours!"

"What about if we do it together," he said. "How would that be?"

"Fine," I replied.

"After three. One, two, three!"

And we pulled off our bags together, then sat, staring at one another.

"You too!" Lampwick said.

"You too!" I cried.

And then, I don't know why, but I started laughing at him—remember he did look ridiculous—and he started laughing at me. We were soon hysterical with laughter, crying with it, tears pouring down our cheeks.

We couldn't even stand up we were giggling so much.

We were on our knees, hooting with laughter, when I realized my knees weren't my own knees any more—they were *donkey's* knees, *donkey's* legs, *donkey's* hooves.

Lampwick was sprouting legs too, and his back was long and gray and hairy. He was growing hair all over, and I was too. But worst of all, there was something sprouting from his rear end—a tail, a scrawny gray tail!

Suddenly we weren't laughing any more, we were crying, sobbing, wailing, and even that didn't sound right.

It came out like this: *Eee Aw! Eee Aw! Eee Aw!*

We were donkeys, donkeys through and through, total donkeys.

CHAPTER ELEVEN

Dance, you donkey, dance!

Caw! Caw! Caw!

It wasn't a crow laughing at us, it was the Little Fat Man, the wagon driver who had brought us to the Land of Toys. He was standing there in the doorway, hands on his hips, laughing his head off at us.

"*Caw! Caw!* Oh dear, oh dear. What do you think you look like! I must say, you bray extraordinarily well, and your ears are marvelously long, and you are exceptionally ugly too, even for donkeys. You're just like all the other silly children I bring to the Land of Toys. You all became donkeys in the end.

"And do you know why? Money, money, money. It's impossible to sell children, but donkeys—that's a different story. Ugly you might be, but you are useful. Did you know a donkey like you can carry nine times his own weight? He may drop dead from overwork, but no one will care. He can bray all he likes, no one will listen. It's my trade, you silly boys. All I do is change boys into donkeys. It's not difficult and I make a fortune out of it, believe you me. All I have to do now is brush you up and take you to market."

The Little Fat Man with the ferret eyes and the cackling laugh that sent shivers down my spine turned out to be nothing but a child stealer. But I knew, even as he dragged Lampwick and me down the street toward the market, that it was all our own fault. He could never have stolen us in the first place if we hadn't been stupid enough to believe him.

The crowd were jeering at us now. "Look at them! Big ears!" they cried. The Little Fat Man poked and prodded us on the way to the market square.

My poor little Pinocchio. My poor Pinocchio, came a small voice in my head. It was my dear sister's voice. Despite all I had done, my Good Fairy hadn't deserted me.

That sweet sound gave me some hope as we were driven into an auction ring and Lampwick was sold off at once to a red-faced farmer. We brayed our goodbyes at each other.

"I am so sorry, Pinocchio," Lampwick brayed. "Still friends?"

"Still friends,"
I brayed back.
"Always. Good luck,
Lampwick."

"Good luck, Pinocchio," he replied, and he was gone.

As for me, I was bought by a circus owner in a black top hat and a twirly moustache, whose dancing horse had just died.

"A dancing donkey," he said, leading me away. "Now that would be something different. No one in the circus world has ever had a dancing donkey."

"But I can't dance," I told him.

"Oh, you will, dear donkey. You will! By the time

I have finished with you, you'll be able to dance the foxtrot, the waltz, the samba, rock and roll. You will do all the tricks I want you to."

"I won't," I brayed. "I won't."

But as it turned out, he was right and I was wrong.

All I cared about in the weeks that followed was to have enough food and water to live on, and to get through each day without a whipping, and that hardly ever happened.

My cruel master, who went by the name of Signor Carpaccio, knew donkeys very well. So if I was ever stubborn or disobedient—and I was all the time to start with—he'd take away my hay and leave my water bucket empty; and if I was still not cooperative, then he'd beat me savagely, cursing at me as he did so, calling me all manner of horrible names.

If I turned my back in order to kick him, he'd whip me. If I tried to run away, he'd whip me. So in the end I did what he wanted me to do and I learned to dance. I learned to do all his tricks.

It took three long months to train me, and all the while I was becoming thinner and thinner. By the end I did as he said I would, I danced the foxtrot, the waltz, the samba and rock and roll—all of which, actually, I grew to like, rock and roll especially. I was really good at that!

And I have to confess, I did feel quite proud when I saw my name up in lights above the Big Top tent, and posters of me dancing all over the town. *"Come and see Pinocchio, the world-famous, amazing, unique, incredible, dancing donkey."* And there I was decked out in my circus finery, a plume of costume feathers on my head, a Turkish carpet over my back and my tail and mane braided with scarlet ribbons.

The Big Top was packed for my first performance, standing room only. Signor Carpaccio strutted around the ring wearing white breeches and a black top hat, his horrible whip in hand. And then to a roll of drums, I trotted out into the spotlight.

"Here he is," Signor Carpaccio announced. "Pinocchio, the most famous donkey in the world, trained by my good self and trained, I assure you, with love and kindness, to dance for you tonight. I must ask you during the performance to keep silent, so that he hears my whispered words of command."

The crowd hushed. "Walk on, Pinocchio," he whispered. And then in an even lower whisper, "Do just as I say, Pinocchio, or you will end up as donkey salami. You'll be dried, then sliced very thinly. Delicious with a gherkin!"

After that, I did exactly as he said.

I walked on.

"Kneel, Pinocchio, say hello to your audience."

I had sliced salami in my head and eyes only for the cruel whip.

I knelt.

"Trot. Gallop. Walk. Stand still."

The music began. "And one, two, three: waltz."

Still I had sliced salami in my head and eyes only for the cruel whip. I waltzed.

The music changed. "Now into the foxtrot. Is he not the most obedient dancing donkey the world has ever known?"

Again the music changed. "And now for his finale, his *pièce de résistance*, Pinocchio shall dance rock and roll."

And so I did, but by now I'd forgotten the cruel whip altogether, and the sliced salami. I danced because I loved the rhythm of the music. I danced because I saw from the faces of the audience all around me that they loved to watch me dance.

Suddenly a gunshot rang out.

The music stopped.

The crowd gasped.

I knew what to do—I fell to the ground and lay still, still as death.

A single cry of horror rang out. "Oh, my poor Pinocchio."

I opened one eye. It was my Good Fairy! She was there in the front row of the audience, hand to her mouth, tears streaming down her face. "No! No!" she cried.

I jumped to my feet and set off, galloping across the ring toward her, braying my heart out. In a flash, Signor Carpaccio was chasing after me, whipping me so hard that I tripped and fell, crashing against the side of the circus ring, where I lay helpless. As he whipped and cursed me, the crowd rose to their feet and booed, but he paid them no attention.

"I'll teach you to disobey," he raged. "I'll teach you to run off."

All the while I was hoping that my Good Fairy would come to my rescue. But when I looked up again, she wasn't there!

I must have imagined her.

Wishful thinking, that's all it had been.

There was no hay and no water for me that night in my stable. And the next day I could barely walk. Signor Carpaccio called in the vet, who examined me. He shook his head slowly. "This donkey will never dance again."

"Then what use is he to me?" said Signor Carpaccio.

And that same afternoon he hauled me through the streets to the market to sell me. "Not even enough meat on you to make you into salami," he grumbled. "You're nothing but skin and bone."

I limped along as best I could, but it was never fast enough for him. "Faster, faster, you useless donkey!" he cried, whipping me on. By the time I reached the market, I was barely able to stagger into the sales ring.

Of course, no one wanted to buy me. Signor Carpaccio was asking four guineas for me, four guineas that no one was willing to pay.

In the end I was sold off for four pennies. My new owner led me away. I didn't care who he was or what he would do with me. At least I wouldn't end up as thinly sliced donkey meat. *Nothing and no one could have been worse than Signor Carpaccio*, I thought. Wrong again, Pinocchio!

"I don't want you for dancing," said my new owner,

leading me along the cliff path out of town. The sea was surging against the rocks below and I felt sick to my stomach—I never did like heights, as a puppet or as a donkey. "No, no, no," he went on. "I want you for your skin, Pinocchio. Donkey skins, properly dried and stretched, make the best drumheads in the world."

He patted my neck, and stroked my back. "You'll do. You'll make a very nice drum-skin, maybe two. I hear you like rock and roll," he continued. "Soon you'll be a drum in a rock and roll band, imagine that! Think of the pleasure you will give.

"But first," he said, as he tied a long rope to one of my back legs, "you will go for a swim, a long, deep swim. You'll have a nice long drink of lovely seawater and when I pull you out you'll be a dead donkey, a drowned donkey, a donkey no more."

With that, he gave me a great
push, and down I went over the
cliff edge, down into deep blue
water, down to the seabed
where the seaweed floated up
around me, where fish came to
gawp at me, where I could not
breathe.

What a way to go, I thought.
What a way to end up, stretched
over a drum, and being thumped
and beaten. *You live and learn,*
I thought. Then I thought again.
*No, you don't! You don't live,
Pinocchio, not any more. You
die!*

I can't be sure exactly how it happened of course, but I have had a long time to think about it, and to try and figure it all out. It is certain that I went into the sea as a living, breathing donkey, and when I woke up

some while later, I wasn't a donkey any more, I was a puppet. All I know is that I woke up inside the stomach of the Giant Gruesome Shark.

Here is what I believe must have happened. If you've got a better idea of what happened to me, then let me know. All I know is that I'm alive to tell the tale.

So, I was pushed off a high cliff by a thoroughly unpleasant drum-maker. I remember nothing from the moment I hit the water—I must have been knocked unconscious. But I woke up some time later sitting in the stomach of the aforementioned Giant Gruesome Shark.

How do I know it was the shark? Because I was told so by a huge fish, a helpful tuna fish, I found in there with me.

"We are in here together, little puppety person, you and me, swallowed in one gulp. You came in as a donkey and went off to be digested; he clearly didn't think I was worth bothering about—too busy dealing with a donkey to bother with a fish. All I heard was lots of grinding and groaning, and when the digestion was done, there was no sign of a donkey, but what I see before me now, a little puppety person."

"My name is Pinocchio," I told him.

"Shhh! Not so loud," whispered the Helpful Tuna Fish. He mustn't know I'm here, or he may want to digest me too."

In spite of the danger I was clearly in, I can't tell you how relieved I was to be myself again. I checked out my legs and arms and knees and elbows to make sure everything was fine. Miraculously, it seemed I was in perfect working order.

"Are we alone in here?" I asked the Helpful Tuna Fish, and I noticed then my voice was echoing. Even if I whispered, the echoes seemed to go on forever as if we were in a vast cave. This was a truly massive monster of a shark.

"I think so," whispered the Helpful Tuna Fish. "It's just you and me, and a lot of smelly bones."

It was true—the bottom of the shark's stomach was littered with rotting fish bones.

"How are we going to get out?" I asked him.

"Now that may be difficult, little Pinocchio," he

replied. "If I remember rightly, I think we came in that way…." He pointed into the dark distance.

"If that was the way in, then it's probably the way out too—stands to reason," I said. "I think I saw a glimmer of light a while ago, maybe the monster opened his mouth?"

"Well, I'd quite like to get out as soon as possible—before he thinks about digesting me. Shall we go, little Pinocchio?"

And so the two of us set forth across the vast, bony wasteland of the shark's stomach, searching for a way out.

CHAPTER TWELVE

from a very smelly place to a better place altogether

The shark's stomach rumbled like thunder, and it stank too, like—well, like a shark's stomach. There never was a shark as humongously huge as this. And there never was a stomach like this, either.

Together, the Helpful Tuna Fish and I struggled on through murky stinking water. He helped me to swim through the deeper water, and I dragged him on when it was too shallow for him to swim. We only kept going, I think, because the pinprick of light at the far end of the shark's stomach beckoned us on. It was our only hope.

As we drew closer the light flickered and glowed more strongly. But it wasn't daylight as I had at first supposed.

It was candlelight. We could see it flickering.

We hurried on, the Helpful Tuna Fish and I, until we came upon a table with a candle on it, stuck in a glass bottle.

And at the table sat an old man, his head in his hands, sobbing.

"Oh, my poor little Pinocchio," he cried. "What has become of you?"

My heart leapt. I knew that voice. I knew that man. It was dear old Gepetto. It was my Papa.

I ran helter-skelter through the shallows, leaping

over the rotting bones, calling out to him as I came,
"I'm here, Papa! Here I am!"

He was on his feet now, holding out his arms in
disbelief, and then he was hugging me, kissing me,
touching my face. "Is it really you, Pinocchio? I am
not dreaming?"

"If you are dreaming, Papa, then I am dreaming too," I replied. "And I'm not."

"Are you sure?" he asked. "I couldn't bear it if this was all just some wonderful dream."

I kicked him on his shin with my sharp little foot.

"Did that hurt, Papa?" I asked.

"Aiee! Ow! Yes! Yes! It hurt! It hurt!" he cried. "I was never so happy to be hurt in all my life. So you are real, Pinocchio. I have found you at last."

"Sshh!" whispered the Helpful Tuna Fish. So we shushed.

When we had stopped our hugging and crying, I told him my story. It took a while, as you can imagine—I mean, think of all the adventures I'd had: the Talking Cricket, the Puppet Theatre, the Blind Cat and the Lame Fox, the Good Fairy with the sea-blue hair who had become my dear sister, my time in prison, my life as a donkey and now this humongous stinky shark.

After I had finished, I introduced Papa to the Helpful Tuna Fish who had been waiting politely all this time.

"It's quite a story, isn't it," said the Helpful Tuna Fish.

"Well, you should hear mine," said Papa.

And so we did.

It wasn't nearly as interesting as my own and I know the Helpful Tuna Fish felt the same because he could hardly stop himself from yawning. Apparently, Papa had left Mama at home and gone off searching for me high and low, all over, everywhere, and he hadn't found me—which was why it wasn't very interesting—and he took an awfully long time telling it.

"And so I set sail across the sea to look for you,"

Papa went on, "and before I know it a storm blows up and I'm tossing around in the waves and what happens? Along comes this huge shark and swallows me whole, me and the boat."

"What, whole?" I asked.

"Mast, sails, oars and stores. Everything, and me in it. So here I've been in this wretched pit of a stomach for two long years. I live on whatever little wiggly fish I can catch. This is my last candle. I've used up all the others from the ship. After this we'll be in the dark."

"Then," said the Helpful Tuna Fish quietly, "may I suggest most politely, before both you and I get horribly digested, that we stop swapping stories and get out of here?"

"How?" Papa asked.

"We go out the same way we came in, Papa," I

said. "Out of his stomach, up through his throat, past his teeth. We'll wait until he opens his huge mouth and then hop and swim out."

"But I can't swim," Papa said.

"We'll help you," said the Helpful Tuna Fish and I together.

And so that's what we did.

Papa was weak and often fell to his knees in the murky water, but we were always there to lift him to his feet. Up out of the darkness of the stomach we struggled, up through the narrow gorge of the throat we climbed, and all the while the monster rumbled and snored in his sleep.

We could smell the salty sea as we reached his tongue. We tiptoed now so as not to wake him up, slowly, slowly toward the light, his sharp white teeth

like jutting cliffs on either side. And then we were sitting on the tip of his great jaw, the dark sea surging around us, the stars bright in the sky.

"Follow me," whispered the Helpful Tuna Fish, and away he swam.

"Hop on my back, Papa, and hold tight around my neck," I said. "I'll swim us home."

"Oh, Pinocchio," said Papa in my ear. "Can you imagine Mama's face when we walk in that door?"

"Soon we won't have to imagine it, Papa," I told him. "Soon we shall see her with our own eyes, both of us back from the dead."

"I think," said the Helpful Tuna Fish as politely as he could, "that it might be better if you stopped talking and saved your strength for swimming. It's a long way to the shore. You're not home yet."

So we swam, each taking a turn to give Papa a ride.

And the Helpful Tuna Fish was right—it was a long way and the truth is we'd never have made it without him. When the sea tossed and tumbled us, or when a terrible storm thundered and crackled above us, so that every ounce of our strength and courage failed, we caught hold of the Helpful Tuna Fish's tail and he swam us through.

It was almost dawn before we saw the lights of the shore, and daylight by the time the Helpful Tuna Fish brought us safely to the beach.

I knelt down and kissed him.

"How can I ever thank you?" I said.

"Maybe by not ever eating tuna fish," he said. "That would be nice. Goodbye, dear Pinocchio."

"Never," I shouted after him. "I shall never eat

tuna fish, I promise."

And that's one promise I have always kept, by the way. That's something I learned in the end: always to keep my promises. And I promise I'll finish the story soon—I know it's gone on a bit.

So, to cut a long story short, after many long months of wandering, Papa and I found our way home. But by the time we got there we weren't alone.

Along the way we met the Lame Fox and the Blind Cat, not lame or blind at all, of course. They confessed at once to dressing up as bandits and tricking me and beating me and hanging me up so that my gold coins would fall out. This surprised me greatly, I must say. They said how truly sorry they were for all the harm they had done me, and begged for my forgiveness.

To be honest, I didn't feel like forgiving them at all, not at first, but I had learned to listen to that little voice in my head, the voice of my Good Fairy, who said that I should. *We all make mistakes, Pinocchio,* she told me, *or had you forgotten?*

And along with us too hopped the Talking Cricket, who was still full of advice and a bit of a chatterbox, not a good traveling companion, but wise, I knew that now. There were moments when I felt like throwing a stick at him, but the Good Fairy whispered in my head, *No, Pinocchio, no.*

And I did as she said.

Not far from home, we came across a farmer beating a donkey by the side of the road. The poor beast was lying half dead in the gutter. I snatched the stick out of

the farmer's hand, and chased him off down the road, kicking him on his backside with my sharp little feet. And yes, you've guessed it, that poor donkey turned out to be my old friend Lampwick.

Papa and I tended his wounds, gave him some water and got him up on his feet again, leading him slowly up the road toward Naples, toward our home at long last.

We were a strange cavalcade: Papa, me, the Talking Cricket, the Lame Fox, the Blind Cat and my friend Lampwick, now a shaggy gray donkey.

There was Mama waiting at the door to greet us. She caught me up in her arms and we hugged and hugged. And who should I see beside her but my dear, loving sister, my Good Fairy with the sea-blue hair!

Everyone I loved in the world was there. I was home at last.

Some dreams do come true, after all.

Well, now you know the true story of Pinocchio, and you know it was true because you heard it from me, and I was there every step of the way. And I didn't change into a boy at all at the end. Of course I didn't.

How could I? Why should I?

Puppet I was. Puppet I am.

And I'm glad I'm not a boy. You see, if I'd been a boy, I'd have grown old. Puppets never grow old. And do we live and learn?

Well, in the end, maybe, sometimes. I'm not quite such a "wooden-head" as I was—or I hope I'm not. My Good Fairy still whispers to me from time to time, drops gentle hints to remind me that everyone matters, reminds me always to be kind.

But I'm here to tell you this.

Puppet I may be, but I'm just like you, whether you're a boy or a girl. We're all the same inside, and no one pulls our strings!

Right?!